LOVE RESCUES ROSANNA

Lord Melton bowed his head. "I am in your debt, Lady Rosanna. Indeed, I have something of yours I must return."

Rosanna looked at him in puzzlement as he reached into his breeches pocket and pulled out a small, crumpled white handkerchief edged with fine lace.

"This is yours, I believe," he said, his eyes sparkling. "You used it to mop my brow and I have kept it by me ever since."

Rosanna stood up and dropped him a small curtsy. "Thank you, sir," she whispered as she held out her hand to take it.

Lord Melton stared down into eyes that were deep and honest.

He was shocked by the flood of emotion he experienced as their fingers touched.

Feelings were racing through him that he had never experienced. But it was far too soon to declare himself to this young woman. And – he realised with a shock – they were alone and unchaperoned and she was no longer his nurse.

THE BARBARA CARTLAND PINK COLLECTION

Titles in this series

LOVE RESCUES ROSANNA

BARBARA CARTLAND

Barbaracartland.com Ltd

THE BARBARA CARTLAND PINK COLLECTION

Barbara Cartland was the most prolific bestselling author in the history of the world. She was frequently in the Guinness Book of Records for writing more books in a year than any other living author. In fact her most amazing literary feat was when her publishers asked for more Barbara Cartland romances, she doubled her output from 10 books a year to over 20 books a year, when she was 77.

She went on writing continuously at this rate for 20 years and wrote her last book at the age of 97, thus completing 400 books between the ages of 77 and 97.

Her publishers finally could not keep up with this phenomenal output, so at her death she left 160 unpublished manuscripts, something again that no other author has ever achieved.

Now the exciting news is that these 160 original unpublished Barbara Cartland books are ready for publication and they will be published by Barbaracartland.com exclusively on the internet, as the web is the best possible way to reach so many Barbara Cartland readers around the world.

The 160 books will be published monthly and will be numbered in sequence.

The series is called the Pink Collection as a tribute to Barbara Cartland whose favourite colour was pink and it became very much her trademark over the years.

The Barbara Cartland Pink Collection is published only on the internet. Log on to www.barbaracartland.com to find out how you can purchase the books monthly as they are published, and take out a subscription that will ensure that all subsequent editions are delivered to you by mail order to your home.

If you do not have access to a computer you can write for information about the Pink Collection to the following address :

Barbara Cartland.com Ltd.
Camfield Place,
Hatfield,
Hertfordshire AL9 6JE
United Kingdom.

Telephone : +44 (0)1707 642629
Fax : +44 (0)1707 663041

THE LATE DAME BARBARA CARTLAND

Barbara Cartland who sadly died in May 2000 at the age of nearly 99 was the world's most famous romantic novelist who wrote 723 books in her lifetime with worldwide sales of over 1 billion copies and her books were translated into 36 different languages.

As well as romantic novels, she wrote historical biographies, 6 autobiographies, theatrical plays, books of advice on life, love, vitamins and cookery. She also found time to be a political speaker and television and radio personality.

She wrote her first book at the age of 21 and this was called *Jigsaw*. It became an immediate bestseller and sold 100,000 copies in hardback and was translated into 6 different languages. She wrote continuously throughout her life, writing bestsellers for an astonishing 76 years. Her books have always been immensely popular in the United States, where in 1976 her current books were at numbers 1 & 2 in the B. Dalton bestsellers list, a feat never achieved before or since by any author.

Barbara Cartland became a legend in her own lifetime and will be best remembered for her wonderful romantic novels, so loved by her millions of readers throughout the world.

Her books will always be treasured for their moral message, her pure and innocent heroines, her good looking and dashing heroes and above all her belief that the power of love is more important than anything else in everyone's life.

"I write about the wonderful glorious moment when men and women fall in love, which is a time in everyone's life that can never be forgotten and is treasured forever."

Barbara Cartland

CHAPTER ONE

William, the new Earl of Melton, stood in the bright sunlight of a July morning, surveying the beautiful thoroughbred horses being paraded around the stable yard at Melton Castle.

At thirty years of age, tall, with dark brown eyes and thick, black unruly hair, it was no wonder that William was considered to be the catch of the Season for any young girl who was anxious to be married.

"I say, old chap, that one looks a bit lively!" Viscount Blackwood, a short, plump young man stood at his side, his green jacket buttoned tightly across his prominent stomach, his face red and shiny, showing the excesses of too much drink the night before.

A large black stallion was snorting and dancing at the end of a leading rein, his eyes rolling as the groom tried to calm him.

"I so agree, George. Far too much of handful even for our brave William."

The speaker was Lady Verity Blackwood, his sister, a tall, elegant woman, dressed in the very latest fashion. She was holding a lacy white parasol and peered up at the Earl through long silky lashes.

Verity Blackwood was noted for her outstanding beauty. The success of the Season, every gentleman in the gathering places of the elite amongst Society was keen to make her acquaintance.

They raved over her lustrous chestnut hair and deep green eyes – unaware that most women observed in whispers amongst themselves that she had a thin, mean mouth and an even meaner and sharper way of speaking when she did not get her own way.

From the moment Verity had met Lord Melton, she had been determined to become his wife. It was easy to be often in his company as her brother was one of the Earl's closest friends.

George Blackwood had travelled all over Europe with William before he inherited the title on the death of his father. They had cut a broad swathe through Society, fond of gambling, horse racing and carousing.

But now they were home in England, William had become Lord Melton, the Castle was his home and Verity could see the prize she had longed for almost within her reach at last.

But pushing the Earl to the point of proposing marriage had proved to be difficult. Now, however, she felt she was nearly there. One last effort to capture his affections and she could start planning the wedding of the year. Indeed, she intended it to be the wedding of the decade!

Lord Melton turned now and smiled at her. A superb rider, he was quite convinced that there was not a horse bred he could not control.

He had been riding since he was three and was well known for his dash and courage when out hunting or racing in a point-to-point.

Since the year before he had inherited the title and estate from his father, the Earl had spent a great deal of time and money buying the best racehorses in the country, even travelling as far as France and Italy to study breeding.

And he certainly did not intend to look foolish and back down in front of his guests, especially Verity, the woman he had almost decided to make his wife.

"Here, John!" he called to the groom. "Throw a saddle over Demon and I *will* take him out."

"Beggin' your pardon, my Lord, but Demon's in a rare black old mood today."

John Barker fought to hold the stallion's head down, dodging the hooves that were kicking sparks out of the cobblestones.

"Really, William, you run a very lax establishment. Your staff seem to express ideas and comments above their station," Verity drawled. "Or perhaps they think you are incapable of handling such a beast."

She laid a lace gloved hand on his arm and added, "I would not want you to risk your life in any way if their estimation of your skills are correct."

"He might have a point, old boy," Viscount Blackwood said. "I say, let's go in and enjoy some breakfast. Bacon and kidneys, nice slice of game pie?"

The Earl frowned. He knew in his heart of hearts that the groom was right. He could see the flecks of sweat flying off the horse's shining black coat. But a challenge had been made and he had never backed away from a challenge in all of his life and he never would. Never!

He pulled off his dark blue jacket and threw it on the ground. The muscles under his thin linen shirt rippled as he took the rein from Barker and with one lithe leap was astride Demon.

Within seconds he had to admit he was in the wrong.

The horse was still half broken, almost wild. He spun round, rearing, fighting the lean legs gripping his sides.

The Earl struggled to get the stallion's head under

control, but the bridle was a light-weight one, used for exercising, not riding.

He still might have succeeded, but suddenly, from out of the cottage next door to the stables, shot a little white puppy.

Shrieking, it fled under the flashing hooves to the safety of the stable beyond. And after it came John Barker's little daughter.

Three years old and running to rescue her pet, her yellow flowered pinafore was a flapping flag in the horse's eyes as she ran straight towards the deadly hooves.

"Millie! Watch out! Stop!"

The Earl knew that he had to save the child whatever the cost! With all his strength, he urged Demon to turn.

Then, with Verity's screams ringing out, the stallion slipped and fell onto the cobbles, crashing down with William, the Earl of Melton, crushed beneath him.

*

Drawn by four smart bay horses, the dark green Donnington carriage moved swiftly through the quiet streets of London.

It was five in the morning and by that time Lady Rosanna Donnington had, she felt, regained her composure. Her breath no longer came in little gasps and the shaking in her hands had almost ceased.

She leant back wearily, her blonde hair shining like spun sugar against the dark upholstery.

Rosanna loosened the jacket of her amber travelling suit, her fingers trembling slightly as they fought with the little bone buttons.

She was beginning to wonder if she had been wise to set off on this venture without Edie, her young maid, but she had given the girl permission to visit her parents in a distant part of London and the maid still had not returned when Rosanna had rung for Henry to bring the carriage round and set off for the country.

Rosanna had left her a note instructing her to travel to Donnington Hall as soon as she returned.

She was lucky that Edie could read. Rosanna's own dear Mama had taught her.

Lady Donnington had believed that everyone should be able to study the Bible and write their own name in a fair hand.

When the young girl, Edie, had arrived at the London house to serve as a scullery maid, Lady Donnington was determined that she should learn the basics of the English language.

Rosanna bit her lip and gazed out into the dark city. Only the occasional flicker of a candle or oil lamp from an upper window broke through the shadows of the city streets.

She knew that travelling alone at night was not how a lady should behave in any circumstances, but she felt she had been given no choice.

'And all this upset, all this grief has been caused by one man – Sir Walter Fenwick!' Rosanna thought angrily. 'How I hate him.'

She had been deeply disturbed this evening at a fashionable party when Sir Walter, whom she had known only slightly but for some time, had amazingly asked her to marry him.

Rosanna had never for one moment thought of such a possibility and the shock combined with a sense of being trapped by this man, had sent her running from the party, oblivious of how it appeared to her hostess.

Now she realised that she should have stayed and courteously made Sir Walter understand that, although she was honoured by his kind offer, it was not only a surprise but that she was not prepared to consider marriage to anyone for the time being. She needed time for quiet reflection following her mother's death.

Sir Walter Fenwick had found her on her own in the gardens, admiring the fountain that cascaded charmingly into a lily pond where small golden fish glided between the pink flowers.

He had pressed a glass of chilled champagne into her hand and standing far too close had said,

"I suggest that we marry very soon, Lady Rosanna. We will be extremely happy together, my dear. We like the same things. I know you love the country and so do I, yet you enjoy yourself in London, as I do."

Ignoring her stunned expression, he continued, "I will make you very happy, Lady Rosanna. We will entertain and be the toast of the countryside. I have great plans for developing the delightful gardens at the house you have inherited. And I long to try out my horses on the Racecourse your uncle built. Ah, Donnington Hall! It will soon become the dream home I have wanted for so long."

Rosanna could hardly believe what she was hearing.

Although, to be fair, it was more or less what she had already heard three times from other gentlemen since her Great-Uncle Leonard had died.

In fact, she had begun to think that every man she met would eventually ask her to be his wife, not for her sake, but her fortune.

Sir Walter's proposal had, though, shocked her more than most. He was not a young man – he would never see forty again.

Stocky in build and only an inch taller than she was, his sandy hair was combed across a very pink scalp in a most unappealing fashion.

He had small grey eyes set close together and his lips

were fleshy and glistened where he licked them continually.

Admittedly he dressed well and, in very small doses, could be quite good company.

But Rosanna considered him vain and opinionated and had heard that as a single gentleman, he lived for his enjoyment of London Society.

Until recently he had never shown the slightest interest in Rosanna. But matters were different now.

It was all a question of money.

'Money, money, money!' she told herself as the horses began to slow as Henry, the coachman, guided them carefully through the poorer, narrower streets on the outskirts of the city.

She sighed. 'What *can* I do if every man I meet wants to marry me because I am rich?'

Unfortunately her vast inheritance had been reported in all the newspapers.

Rosanna had always known that her great-uncle, Sir Leonard Donnington, was a rich man. But he disliked Society and any social invitations he received, he refused.

A recluse for many years, even from his family, he had stayed resolutely in the country, happy with his house and estate.

He lived for his gardens and greenhouses where he perfected the cultivation of rare orchids.

But most of all his pride and joy was the perfect little Racecourse he had built in the grounds of Donnington Hall, so that he could train his horses in private.

Rosanna had been wholly unaware that she would one day inherit Sir Leonard's fortune.

She had not seen him very often, but on the rare occasions when, as a small child, she had been taken to visit him, she had liked the small, shy man who enjoyed showing her the latest exotic flower he was cultivating in one of his greenhouses.

Rosanna's father, the late Earl of Donnington, had been a generous, kind-hearted soul who had believed every hard luck story that he was told. No beggar left the back door without a half-sovereign in his pocket. No charity applied for funds without receiving double their request.

Just after Rosanna had been born, her father had invested all his wealth in a South African gold mine that failed to produce a single nugget of gold.

He had then been forced to sell the family home, Donnington Hall to his uncle, Sir Leonard, and the Earl and his wife had moved to a small house in London.

When her father died, Rosanna had been left a small sum of money while her brother, Clive, had inherited nothing but the family silver and the title.

Then a stray bullet in a skirmish in a far away land had ended her beloved brother's life, as he fought in the regiment he loved so much.

'Oh, Clive, why did you have to die?' Rosanna murmured to herself, as the carriage picked up speed. They had left the last few houses behind and were now heading out into the dark sleeping countryside.

'If you were still alive, none of this would be happening to me.'

Clive had never married so on his death, Rosanna and her mother had been left with enough income to keep them comfortable, if not in the height of fashion.

They lived in a small house in a quiet part of Mayfair, kept a few servants and a carriage and were invited out to several parties which took place during the Season.

Then tragedy had struck and the smiling face of fate had turned to a frown. Rosanna's beloved Mama had caught a chill that turned into a fever.

Although Rosanna had cared for her devotedly for weeks with the help of a nurse, Lady Donnington had died, leaving her daughter all alone in the world – except for her great-uncle.

Sir Leonard had sent a letter of condolence and a brief note stating that as soon as she felt able to travel, she must come to Donnington Hall for a visit. And a grieving Rosanna had written back, formally promising to do so.

However, only two months later, just after her twenty-first birthday and without any warning, Sir Leonard, too, had died – and her whole life changed overnight.

She had been astonished to learn that he had left her his whole estate – house, grounds and fortune.

Rosanna had also discovered to her utter amazement that her great-uncle had been an exceptionally rich man. Unlike his nephew, he had invested wisely over the years and had even enlarged Donnington Hall, so that it could contain all the treasures he had accumulated.

Rosanna had felt almost overwhelmed by what she had unexpectedly inherited.

She wondered how at just twenty-one years old, she could possibly deal with so much money.

More important was how she could spend it not only on herself, but to help other people.

What she had not anticipated nor imagined for a moment was that the story of her inheritance would so quickly reach the long ears of London Society.

To her surprise she found herself asked to select gatherings, where people who had either ignored her or given her a mere nod when they had met before, now embarrassed her with invitation after invitation.

Men who had never given her a second glance in the past, who as far as she could remember, had never even asked her to dance, now laid their hearts and souls at her feet.

'I had received three offers of marriage to consider before I set out this evening,' she told herself, 'and this is the fourth. Is it possible that any young man could be so ridiculous as to think that having more or less cold shouldered me since we first met, I will now fall into his arms like a ripe plum the moment he holds them out to me?

'It's my money they want to marry, not me!' she sighed, swaying as the carriage rocked from side to side as they rounded a sharp bend. 'If anyone else asks me, I will scream.'

She knew deep down, however, that she would do nothing of the sort. That would be bad manners and as her mother had once said to her as she grew older,

"Remember when a man asks you to marry him, darling, he is offering you himself and everything he possesses and hopes for in the future. Therefore the greatest compliment any woman can receive is for a man to ask her to be his wife."

"What do you say, Mama," Rosanna had enquired, "if you dislike him and you have no wish to marry him?"

Her mother had smiled. "Even if you dislike him, you must always be charming and never unpleasant."

"What do you mean?"

"You must be kind and understanding if you want to say 'no'. At the same time leave him feeling that he has not been insulted, but merely been told in a friendly fashion that he is charming, delightful and pleasant, but for the moment at any rate, you have no wish to marry anyone."

But now the men who had offered her their hearts and their names had somehow left her breathless and just a little frightened.

They had told her in no uncertain terms that they were determined to make her the happiest woman in the world and the fierce glare in their eyes was quite alarming.

"I love you from the top of your head to the soles of your dear little feet," one man had told her. "We will be blissfully happy. I want to travel all over the world and I am sure you will enjoy seeing the countries as much as I will."

His voice had dropped as he continued, "and we will add glorious items to your glorious house."

Rosanna had frowned. She had no inclination to add anything to her life at present, especially a man who would marry her not because he believed she was the perfect woman chosen for him by Heaven itself, but because she now possessed what he had always wanted.

'They love what I have in the bank,' she muttered, staring out of the carriage window at where the pale apricot light of dawn was painting the eastern sky. 'I am only the gate leading into the orchard, not the orchard itself.'

And her brilliant blue eyes filled with tears.

As the horses cantered on, she thought how, ever since she was small, she had hoped that one day she would find a man she loved and who loved her completely, because she was who she was, not what she possessed.

The coach rumbled over a wooden bridge and Rosanna wiped tears from her pale cheeks.

'Yes, I felt so lucky then,' she sniffed. 'Dear Mama was still alive. No man tried to persuade me to marry him while she was there to protect me.'

But now Rosanna was completely alone in the world.

Alone, unprotected and very, very rich.

There were no relatives to help her. The solicitors in London who had handled her inheritance were kind but elderly men. Once the money had been paid into her bank, they had no further need to offer her assistance.

Oh, if only her great-uncle had lived long enough to guide her as to how to handle his fortune.

"I hope she will do her best to carry on the family traditions and make her life as significant and useful as I would want it to be," he had written in his will.

It seemed to Rosanna as if the house and the money which at first had been a delight to her were now a millstone she wanted to forget and ignore.

'Great-Uncle Leonard wanted me to achieve something in my life,' she told herself. 'The money is a burden, but one I must carry. I must find a way to do some good in the world, and being forced into marriage is not the right way."

"I hate it!" she cried out loud. "I want to be married for myself. I want to find love, the real love which is different in every way from what they are offering me."

The question was, where would she find it?

Just then the first rays of the sun shot through the carriage window.

Rosanna took a deep breath. A new day. What would it bring her? Last night, scared and unhappy, she had fled back to her Mayfair house after the party and swiftly packed as much as she could into two valises.

She knew she needed to escape and the only place she could go on her own was Donnington Hall. It was time she inspected her property and surely no one would expect her to travel there alone.

Just then she heard the coachman yelling and the cadence of the horses' hooves changed. It sounded as if one had cast a shoe.

The coach slowed and as Rosanna gazed out of the window, she saw that they were pulling into the courtyard of a prosperous looking inn.

She pulled on her dark travelling cloak, hiding her blonde hair under its hood.

The coachman helped her down. "Sorry, my Lady, the lead horse has cast a shoe. The smithy is just over the road and it will only be an hour or so before we're on our way again."

"Thank you, Henry. I am sure the inn-keeper will provide a private room where I can wait. Indeed, some breakfast would be welcome. Let me know when we are ready to set off once more."

Even as she spoke, the inn-keeper's wife appeared, wiping her hands on her apron, bobbed a respectful curtsy and led her inside.

As Rosanna followed her down a musty passageway towards the stairs to the upper chambers, she hesitated for an instant by an open door.

Inside the room she could see an elegant woman dressed in the latest fashion and a portly young man standing arguing.

Ignored behind them, lying back in a chair with a heavily bandaged leg propped up on a stool, was a tall, rugged man with dark hair.

Rosanna stared. Wrapped in a heavy tweed travelling cloak, his face was pale, his eyes shut and he looked very ill. He groaned as he tossed restlessly in his chair and even from the doorway she could see beads of sweat forming on his brow.

'Poor man,' she thought, her heart aching at the sight of his suffering.

And as she walked on after the landlady, she felt a surge of pity for the invalid who was being so ignored by his companions.

CHAPTER TWO

Rosanna was shown into a small upstairs room, which was plainly decorated with a sullen fire smouldering in the grate.

She pushed back the hood of her dark velvet travelling cloak and sank down onto a chair.

The inn-keeper's wife bobbed another curtsy. "I'm Mrs. Perks, at your service. Can I be fetchin' you somethin' to eat or drink, my Lady? If you've been travelling far – "

Her voice trailed away. Obviously she was anxious to know where the pretty young lady had come from and where she was heading without a chaperone.

Rosanna smiled wearily. She was indeed hungry. She had left London so early in the morning that she had taken nothing to sustain her. She had not wanted to ask her housekeeper, Mrs. Dawkins, for breakfast, because she would have had to explain where she was going.

Instead she had left her a note, saying that she would be in the country if anyone asked for her and could not be reached.

Now she was famished.

"If there is any soup or cold chicken and perhaps a piece of new bread, that would be delightful, thank you, Mrs. Perks," she said, unaware that the beauty of her bright blue eyes and the genuine warmth of her expression had

14

immediately won over the canny older woman.

When she was on her own, Rosanna crossed to the window and knelt on the wooden seat underneath it.

Through the grimy glass, she looked down into the stable yard where she could see her own carriage waiting and next to it a larger, more splendid coach.

There was a coat of arms painted in gold on the dark blue door, but although she rubbed a clean patch in the glass, she could not see any details.

Just then Mrs. Perks bustled back into the room with a tray of food and drink.

"Tell me," Rosanna asked, sitting at the table and admiring the bowl of vegetable soup and platter of cold meat and cheese. "Does the dark blue coach belong to the party I saw downstairs, the invalid gentleman?"

"Oh, yes, my Lady. Indeed it does. That's the Earl of Melton himself! And a nicer gentleman you would be hard to find. Such a tragedy, hurtin' his leg in a riding accident. He's very poorly, my Lady."

Rosanna drank a mouthful of soup and smiled her appreciation at the flavour. "But should he be travelling if he is so ill? Surely his family who are with him should take better care of him."

Mrs. Perks sniffed in disdain and wiped her hands on her apron.

"Beggin' your pardon, my Lady, but I happen to know they're not his family. Just friends. A Viscount Blackwood and his sister Lady Verity Blackwood."

"And no doctor travels with them? For shame!"

"I do believe as how they do be on their way back to the Earl's castle from Bath. They wanted him to take the waters and see a special sort of doctor down there."

Rosanna nodded and thanked Mrs. Perks before

dismissing her. She had not meant to gossip with the woman, but could not help wonder what sort of friends would put a sick man through such an ordeal.

After her meal, Rosanna felt stronger. In the bright light of day, her escape to Donnington Hall seemed a sensible course of action to have taken. There she would be safe from all admirers and could begin to think about her inheritance and all that it would mean.

'Oh, but I am being so remiss,' she said to herself. 'I have eaten well, but has Henry? He has driven all morning and has to attend to shoeing the horse as well.'

Chiding herself for being so self-centred, Rosanna slipped on her cloak, ran down the stairway and gave instructions to a maid to provide food for her coachman.

On her way back upstairs, she passed the doorway to the room where she had seen the invalid Earl and stopped as a groan rang out.

It was followed by another and Rosanna's gentle heart overcame her trepidation at appearing forward.

She pushed open the door and peered inside. The Earl was lying as she had seen him earlier, but his two companions were absent.

'Probably gone to have a meal,' Rosanna thought crossly. 'And left this poor man to his own devices.'

As she watched, the Earl tossed and turned on his chair, obviously in great pain. Beads of sweat clung to his forehead and his dark hair was dishevelled.

Rosanna tiptoed forward, wondering what she could do to help. She knew that being alone with a strange man was not the correct form of behaviour, but still she did not hesitate.

There was a bowl with water on a table at his side. Swiftly, she plucked a handkerchief from her pocket and, soaking it in the water, dabbed gently at his forehead.

The coolness seemed to bring him some relief as the groans ceased and he lay still in the chair.

Rosanna was aware of the breadth of his shoulders under his cloak and the firm contours of his features. It was a strong face, she decided, even if now drawn with pain.

As she turned away to soak her handkerchief once more, the hood of her cloak slipped back and her cloud of fine blonde hair escaped.

"*Angel* – " the word emerged from between his dry lips and Rosanna looked back, startled. She had not realised that the Earl was conscious.

His hand came up, faltering, and touched her cheek. "An *angel* – " he muttered and then slipped back into an uneasy sleep once more.

Rosanna stood gazing down at him, and then gasped as she heard voices coming along the passage. In a second, she had pulled up her hood and slipped out of the door.

She hurried up the stairs, but paused as she reached the bend. She did not want them to hear her footsteps on the wooden treads and know that someone had been in the room.

She could hear their voices clearly now. How dreadful. She was in danger of eavesdropping! Her mother would have been ashamed of her.

"Really, George, I am becoming so tired of all this sickness." It was a woman's voice, hard and unpleasant in tone.

"Oh, come, Verity, William can't help being sick. I thought you and he were – well, you know, waiting for him to come and ask for your hand – "

"Don't be more stupid than you need be, George," the woman snapped. "I have every intention of being William's wife, I just wish his wretched leg would improve and he could return to full health. I am so bored with doing nothing all day but administering to a sick man."

"Hush, lower your voice, sister. He's asleep in there, you know. You might wake him."

Rosanna heard the swish of the woman's dark red gown on the floor.

"Call the servants. We must get William into the coach and take him back to the castle immediately. I shall insist that the doctor finds him a proper nurse."

As they left, Rosanna ran back up the stairs to her refuge.

'Poor man,' she thought. 'To be so ill and helpless. I pity him being cared for by friends like that!'

Minutes later, she watched from the window as the great blue coach trundled out of the courtyard. And ten minutes afterwards, she was informed that her carriage was ready and waiting for her to continue her journey to Donnington Hall.

As the miles sped by under the cantering hooves, Rosanna wondered about her new home and what she would find there.

She knew that her great-uncle had extended it in recent years, but that part of it was very old. Indeed, her mother had once told her that one wing had been a monastery several hundred years ago.

'I know it is now one of the largest and most important houses in this part of the county,' Rosanna mused. 'I wish I could remember more about it.'

Her memories of childhood visits were too vague to be of much use.

Rosanna leant forward and gazed out of the window. The countryside was beautiful with green rolling meadows and blue hills in the far distance.

'Oh, what a marvellous place to ride in,' she cried.

Rosanna was an accomplished equestrienne and she was keen to inspect the horses she now owned and visit the private Racecourse that her great-uncle had built half a mile from Donnington Hall.

'What a strange man he must have been,' she thought. 'Living on his own in a big house with only a few servants for company.'

The solicitors had told Rosanna that the servants were prepared to stay on and take care of Donnington Hall, while she decided what to do with the estate.

It was a comfort to know that someone would be there when she arrived, unannounced and unchaperoned.

She clasped her hands together in excitement as the carriage slowed and from the window she could see they were turning through ornate iron gates being held open by an elderly lodgekeeper.

She had arrived at Donnington Hall!

A fine avenue of giant oak trees curved through green meadows and then, as the carriage rumbled over a little bridge across a sparkling stream, the oak trees ended and she saw ahead of her the house she now owned.

For a moment Rosanna could only gasp because it was so much bigger and so much more impressive than she had ever imagined.

Built of honey coloured stone, it stood at the top of a slope leading down to a lake covered with beautiful yellow and apricot water lilies.

Rosanna could see where the new wing had been added to the old building, but it had been built with great sensitivity.

The many windows glinted in the sunshine and there seemed to be flowers everywhere, red roses and white lilies and cascades of tiny blue blossoms.

"It is quite lovely," she said out loud as her carriage drew up at the impressive entrance.

Even as the horses came to a standstill, the front door opened and she saw an elderly butler was waiting for her to descend.

A groom came running round from the rear of the house and held the horses as Henry jumped down and helped her out.

"Good morning. I am Lady Rosanna Donnington – "

"Yes, my Lady," the butler replied warmly. "I am Bates, your butler. I am pleased to welcome you to Donnington Hall. We have been hoping you would be visiting us ever since we lost Sir Leonard. We have been very lonely without him."

It was not something Rosanna had expected a servant to say.

Before she could think of a reply, Bates said, "shall I instruct your coachman to drive into the stables?"

"Please do," Rosanna replied, finding her voice with some difficulty.

It was all so strange and different from what she had expected.

Bates returned to her side and ushered her into the house. A very impressive entrance hall lay ahead of her, the black and white marble floor gleaming. A grand curving staircase rose up to the first floor gallery.

"If you will come this way, my Lady," Bates said, "I will take you to the drawing room, which I am sure you would like to see first."

"I want to see the whole house," Rosanna told him. "I haven't been here for many years, although I believe I was born here."

"That is true," he agreed. "Begging your pardon, my Lady, but Mrs. Bates and I have often thought it was sad that Sir Leonard had no wish for his family to see what a beautiful home he had created and how magnificent it is in every possible way."

Rosanna drew in her breath. She was already aware that the furniture in the hall was old and valuable and most impressive. The pictures were, she was quite certain, painted by masters of their craft.

When they stopped halfway down the passage, the butler opened the door and she had her first glimpse of what she was to learn later was reported to be the most beautiful room in the house.

It was certainly imposing and almost dazzling in the sunshine streaming in through the long windows.

Rosanna noted that the furniture was exquisite and so were the delicate watercolours hanging on the walls.

The room itself was beautifully proportioned, painted in the very palest green with gold edges to the plaster roses that adorned the ceiling.

"This is the drawing room, my Lady," Bates announced. "Sir Leonard finished collecting these pictures just before he died."

"It is so lovely," Rosanna enthused.

Bates smiled. "I knew you would be pleased," he said.

Rosanna drew in her breath before she asked, "I cannot understand, when he had such a beautiful home, why my great-uncle never wanted visitors."

There was silence before the butler answered,

"When Sir Leonard's wife, Lady Margaret was alive, they enjoyed a very social life. But tragically, as you know, she died in childbirth and after that, well, Sir Leonard withdrew from Society completely. He spent all his time adding to his collections of fine porcelain and paintings.

"He used to say to me, 'Bates, I have lost the most beautiful woman in the whole world, but I can try and collect other beautiful objects to adorn the rooms of her house in her memory'."

Rosanna wiped away a tear that trickled down her cheek.

'Poor Great-Uncle Leonard,' she thought. 'If only Mama and I had realised how unhappy he was, we would have visited more often, I am sure.'

"My wife and I having been with Sir Leonard for so long, we were used to his ways," Bates told her. "But he was content here by himself with his books. He loved his garden and, probably most of all, his racehorses."

For a moment no one spoke and then Bates continued,

"I am sure, my Lady, you would like to see the rest of the house. Or perhaps you would rather wait until after I have served luncheon?"

"No, I would very much like to see it all now," Rosanna replied enthusiastically.

"Then if you will please come this way," Bates invited, "and I will show you your new home."

By the time Rosanna had explored the house from the cellars to the attics, she realised that she would love Donnington Hall as much as her great-uncle had loved it.

It was an enchanting place and although it was big, it still gave her the impression of being a home, not just a house. Each room was beautifully decorated and full of exciting and interesting objects.

Translucent porcelain from China, magnificent statues from India and weird and wonderful carvings from far away islands in the South Pacific.

Finally, when she had inspected the servants' quarters on the top floor, Bates escorted her to where a ladder led through a trap door onto the very roof of the house.

"Would you wish to climb outside, my Lady? It is very steep."

Rosanna hesitated but only for a moment. She wanted to see and explore every inch of her new home and holding up her amber travelling skirt with one hand, she nimbly ran up the ladder onto the roof where a flag pole stood.

She gasped as she gazed out on the magnificent view of the land which now belonged to her. It was only from this height that she could comprehend the magnificence of her inheritance.

Downstairs, her luggage had been taken from the carriage up to what Bates described as the Blue bedroom.

"Sir Leonard used to sleep in the Master bedroom," he told her, "but this room was the one that Lady Margaret used as her private sitting room."

He gestured to a beautiful painting that had caught Rosanna's eye as soon as she entered the room.

"This is a study of Lady Margaret on her twenty-first birthday. Sir Leonard could not bear to hang it in his room, but he would not have it covered up and put away."

Rosanna stared at the lovely face. Lady Margaret was smiling out of the canvas, as if someone she loved very much was standing watching her.

"It is so sad that he never remarried," she said softly.

"That's what my wife thought would happen sooner or later," Bates replied. "But the years passed by and he stayed true to Lady Margaret's memory."

And when Rosanna finally retired to bed that evening, exhausted after her long journey, her dreams were a strange mixture of the great-aunt she had never met and the poor sick Earl she had met at the inn earlier that day.

*

The following morning dawned bright and fine. Rosanna rose refreshed, bathed and discovered that, Jenny, the little maid who was caring for her until Edie arrived, had laid out her riding clothes.

"Mr. Bates was sure you would want to ride one of the horses from the stables," she said.

Rosanna stared at her reflection in the long mirror. The dark blue riding habit suited her admirably.

"He is quite correct. I am keen to explore, especially the Racecourse."

"Oh, it be very fine, my Lady. I am not keen on those great horses myself. Too many teeth and nasty big feet! But Sir Leonard showed all us staff when it was finished."

Rosanna ran down the wide curving staircase. She felt so happy this morning. The sun was shining, she loved Donnington Hall and she was free from her unwanted admirers, especially Sir Walter Fenwick!

Bates watched from a window as the lovely young lady mounted on a pretty little chestnut mare, cantered past with Tom, one of the grooms.

His wife appeared at his shoulder. "She is such a lovely child." She dabbed at her eyes with her apron. "Sir Leonard would have been very proud."

Bates nodded his agreement. "That he would. But she is very young and so alone in the world. Donnington Hall is a big responsibility to place on those slender shoulders."

He turned away with a sigh and went back to his duties.

The Racecourse was grander and much larger than Rosanna had expected. She reined in Taffy, the beautiful chestnut mare she had chosen to ride, and stared in surprise and appreciation at the long circular sweep of grass between the white fences.

"I wonder, my Lady, if they told you that Sir Leonard's horses have won a number of races," Tom said.

"He and his great friend, the late Lord Melton, would send entries to all the big meetings and point-to-points. This is where they trained the horses to run true and jump. Although they were friends, they were great competitors as well."

Rosanna had already inspected the stables and admired the magnificent steeds.

"I believe the present Earl was injured in a riding accident," she ventured, hoping this was not bordering on gossip with a servant.

"Indeed, my Lady. He owns a fiery stallion, name of Demon. No one can ride it but his Lordship, but it threw him a couple of months ago now and damaged his leg badly, so I'm told."

Rosanna turned for home. There was so much to think about, but she decided that when the Earl had recovered his health and strength, she would extend her great-uncle's invitation for the Melton horses to train again at Donnington Hall.

She did not want people to think she was looking for an unfair advantage if she ran her horses against his in future races.

The following day Rosanna spent on horseback exploring every inch of her new estate, meeting the lodge-keeper and his wife, and visiting the tenants of the cluster of little farm cottages.

Everywhere she went she was greeted with friendly smiles. Little children scampered alongside her horse, waving shyly and several of the farmers' wives came out of their cottages to bob their curtsies and offer her cold lemonade or cider.

It was obvious that people had been awaiting her arrival with anxious concern, worried as to how their lives would change now she was in charge.

She could see how the estate had been built up and improved year by year and was only too anxious to assure everyone that she would try and continue in the same way as her great-uncle.

'It is a vast responsibility,' Rosanna thought as she walked Taffy slowly up the driveway. 'But one I have to accept. I will do the very best I can. I trust it will be enough. So many people depend on me now.'

As she neared the house, she saw two carriages moving away from the front door.

'Visitors!' she exclaimed. 'Perhaps they are neighbours leaving calling cards, but I have no wish to be bothered with the social life here until I am more at home than I am at the moment.'

She rode round to the stable block and Tom helped her to dismount before leading Taffy away to her stall.

To Rosanna's dismay, the carriages were there in the courtyard. Obviously they were not local dignitaries coming to pay their respects to the new owner of Donnington Hall.

But perhaps they were business acquaintances of her uncle, come to consult her about some detail of the estate.

Whoever they were, she could not greet them covered in dust and dirt from her day's excursion.

Rosanna slipped indoors via the little room where the flowers for the house were arranged. Crossing the hall to the stairs, she could hear from the laughter and voices in the drawing room that there must be quite a number of visitors.

There was no sign of Bates or the rest of the staff and she imagined that he was serving tea. She knew she could rely on him to do all that was necessary in her absence.

With Jenny's help, she changed swiftly into a pale pink dress, brushed her hair until it shone like polished gold silk and caught it up at the back with a pretty tortoishell comb.

"Do you know who the visitors are, Jenny?" she asked as she put on her pink silk shoes.

"I did hear them say to Mr. Bates that they were friends of yours from London, my Lady. They've brought ever so much luggage."

Rosanna frowned at her reflection in the mirror. Who in the world could it be?

Even as she entered the drawing room, she still had no idea of who awaited her.

She gasped, stunned, for there, standing in front of the fireplace, legs astride, one of the best Sevres teacups lost in his beefy hand, was Sir Walter Fenwick, the man she hated most in all the world. The man she had run away from in such fear.

He had found her!

CHAPTER THREE

Rosanna stared at Sir Walter, overcome by the feelings that flowed through her. This was her worst nightmare come true. All her plans to escape to the country had been in vain. It had never crossed her mind that this dreadful man would follow her to Donnington Hall.

Just for a moment as she stood in the doorway, Sir Walter did not realise she was there. He was laughing at something someone had said.

It was the man who was speaking who exclaimed, "ah, here is our delightful young hostess!"

Sir Walter turned and before Rosanna could move, he had taken both her hands in his and was kissing them.

"We could not stay in London without you, my dear," he said. "The place seemed empty and very boring so we have come to tell you how much we miss you. In fact, *I* do unbearably. Tell me you are pleased to see me."

As he finished speaking, he raised her hands to his lips and kissed them again.

With the greatest difficulty Rosanna pulled away from him.

Walking into the room she saw there were two other girls there, Miranda and Susan de Vere, neither of whom were great friends of hers.

The two younger men, James Heath and Patrick

McNab, she had danced with at various functions. They had been particularly flattering when they had realised how rich she had become.

"I hope you are glad to see us, Lady Rosanna," Patrick said, dusting the remains of a slice of cake from his fancy waistcoat.

"It is certainly a surprise," Rosanna replied dryly.

"We thought when we learnt you had left London that this was where you would be," Sir Walter said, beaming, "and that you might be lonely without us."

There was laughter at this.

Miranda de Vere, a chubby, rather plain girl, came forward and held out her hand. It had been at her birthday dance two nights ago that Sir Walter had asked Rosanna to marry him.

Now she said, "goodness, Rosanna, I am so tired after such a journey. I had no idea your new home was so far away from London. But I suppose if my bedroom here is comfortable, I will not complain."

Rosanna felt a chill run down her back.

Then she asked, "are you thinking of staying?"

"Of course," Sir Walter answered. "I brought Miranda and Susan as chaperones and also two friends who told me the other night how much they admire you."

He paused for a moment before continuing, "I am delighted to see you, Lady Rosanna, and to discover that your home is even finer and more significant than the newspapers reported."

"That is true," James Heath agreed. "I had no idea there was such a magnificent collection of pictures. It makes me very curious to see the rest of Donnington Hall and all the marvels it contains."

Rosanna was about to reply when the door opened and Bates asked, "will you be requiring tea, my Lady?"

As she walked towards him he said in a voice only she could hear,

"I am afraid as these visitors have arrived so unexpectedly, Mrs. Bates is worried about the quantity and quality of the provisions we have in store, my Lady."

Rosanna frowned. "I will see Mrs Bates later. At the moment I am hoping they will all leave very soon."

She turned back to her guests, and then her hand was suddenly taken by Sir Walter, who was standing far too close to her.

He whispered, "how could you have been so cruel as to run away without telling me, little Rosanna? I can hardly believe you would do such a thing. But I have found you and now nothing matters but that we are together again."

Rosanna did not speak. When she felt the pressure of his hot damp hand over hers she wanted to scream.

But this was not the time nor place to have an argument. She pulled her hand free and took the cup Bates was offering her.

The five visitors chatted endlessly about the value of the pictures, the statuary and the beautiful Sevres tea service.

They fingered the beautiful drapes at the windows, ran their hands over the upholstery on the chairs and admired everything in sight.

Everything they said was in very bad taste. It made them sound avaricious, like a flock of crows picking at a dead rabbit by the side of the road.

Eventually Sir Walter said, "you are very quiet, my dear. Anyone would think you are not pleased to see us!"

Rosanna did not answer for a moment. Then she replied in a low voice,

"Sir, I had not expected guests so soon. It is impossible, with no notice, to make you as comfortable as I should want you to be."

"All I wanted," he breathed, "was to be alone with you. But I thought it incorrect for me to arrive without a chaperone. That is why I invited my friends to accompany me."

Rosanna did not answer.

James Heath said, "this is the most amazing house. I am looking forward to exploring it while we are staying with you, Lady Rosanna."

Rosanna took a deep breath. "I am afraid," she ventured slowly, "that you have come too soon. I am not entertaining at Donnington Hall at the moment." She paused for a moment before continuing, "the deaths of my great-uncle and my dear mother make that impossible."

Susan de Vere, who was taller than her older sister and as thin as a rake, raised her plucked eyebrows at Miranda before saying,

"Of course we understand. It is always difficult to entertain when you have had no prior experience."

Sir Walter glared at her for her sniping remark and said, "I think, my dearest Rosanna, that you are worrying unnecessarily. We have come because we anticipated that you would be feeling lonely."

He smiled as he resumed, "we want to help you in every way possible in this enchanting house which you know as well as I do is too large for one small person such as yourself to manage."

For a moment there was silence. Then Rosanna stated, "as I only arrived yesterday, I can hardly plan anything amusing and entertaining."

"All I desire and what I am sure my friends want, is your company," Sir Walter replied. Patting her hand, he rose to his feet. "I am going to talk with your butler and ask him what he can do for us."

Before Rosanna could speak, he was walking towards the door. He had reached it before she managed to cry out,

"Stop! Please stop!"

Sir Walter looked round and called cheerfully, "I cannot allow you to be worried. Leave everything to me."

When he had gone, everyone began to talk at once.

"We thought you were expecting us," Miranda said sitting down in the chair Sir Walter had vacated and taking Rosanna's hand in hers. "Lord, it never crossed my mind that you did not know we were coming."

"I only arrived here yesterday," Rosanna repeated. "The guest beds have not been used for such a long time, indeed, they may even be damp."

She could think of nothing else to make staying at Donnington Hall sound unpleasant.

The girl gave a cry. "We have annoyed you. I know we have! It was stupid of us to listen to Sir Walter, but you know when he wants something, he always gets it. There is no point in arguing with him. Indeed, I would be quite scared to do so."

Rosanna felt her heart sink. She knew however much she might be upset or feel it was impossible for her to entertain visitors until she and the staff were prepared for them, Sir Walter would get his own way.

She knew by the expression on his fleshy face when he returned that she was right.

"It is all arranged," he said, "we may have a dinner which will not be as good as we are accustomed to, but at least there will be something to eat and a bed in which to sleep. I know that our dear hostess would have felt embarrassed if we had felt obliged to return to London."

No one spoke so he carried on,

"My feelings were hurt when she left." He smiled at

her before he added, "in fact, I thought of her all alone perhaps longing for us but unable to say so!"

The way he spoke by softening his voice and the intense stare of his gooseberry green eyes made Rosanna not only angry, but frightened.

'He is planning to have me,' she thought. 'He is determined by hook or by crook to make me his wife. He is so keen to own this house and when he sees the horses and the Racecourse he will be even more determined.'

She managed to slip away to speak to Bates.

"I am desperately sorry to worry you and Mrs. Bates so much," she said. "Especially as I have only just arrived myself."

"That is quite all right, my Lady," he replied. "I knew you were not expecting them."

Rosanna said, "I would never invite guests before giving you and the staff ample warning."

"Well, I am sure we can manage."

Rosanna smiled at him. "Thank you, Bates for being so kind and understanding."

She walked back towards the drawing room and Bates watched her go, a frown on his face. She was such a small girl and so alone in the world.

As she reached the door, he saw Sir Walter appear, like a hawk watching his prey. He towered over Lady Rosanna, holding out his arm and insisting he walked with her back into the room.

To Bates he looked like a gaoler escorting his prisoner to an execution.

He returned to the kitchen a grim expression on his face. He had met men such as Sir Walter before. He knew exactly what he was after and wondered if little Lady Rosanna would be able to hold out against him.

The next morning dawned bright and sunny. Rosanna had slept badly and was wide awake by six o'clock. She washed swiftly before the maid could appear and dressed in her favourite dark blue riding habit.

She slipped downstairs, through the quiet house. Only a couple of housemaids saw her, but she put a finger to her lips to silence their automatic greetings.

Round at the stables, she found much more activity. The stable lads and grooms were already hard at work, cleaning out the stalls and grooming the horses.

Rosanna asked for Taffy, the chestnut mare, to be saddled.

"Beggin' your pardon, my Lady, but shall I accompany you?" Tom, the youngest groom, asked as he helped her mount and handed her the reins.

"No, thank you, Tom. I am sure you have far more pressing duties than to ride with me. I shall not go far and Taffy is quite safe. Oh, and Tom – " she gazed down at the round, honest face – "if Sir Walter wants to ride out – then please tell him there is no suitable horse at present."

Tom nodded thoughtfully, watching her as she trotted out of the stable yard.

Rosanna pushed Taffy into a canter as she crossed the first fields. She was free! Oh, how marvellous to be away from the atmosphere inside Donnington Hall.

She had been sure that Sir Walter would suddenly appear and want to ride with her.

'This is quite dreadful, feeling a prisoner in my own home,' she said to herself as she turned Taffy's head towards the open countryside. 'I wish I could ride and ride until that awful man vanishes back to London.'

She galloped up a steep slope and reined in on the crest of the hill, where she enjoyed a fine view back down to Donnington Hall.

Her blonde hair had escaped from its tight bonds and flowed down over her shoulders. She tossed it back, breathing in the glorious fresh air.

On the other side of the hill, the land stretched ahead for miles and far in the misty distance she could see the faint outline of a castle's battlements with a flag flying high in the early morning sunlight. It looked like something out of a fairy tale and Rosanna sighed.

That was where the poor Earl of Melton lived, she realised. How she envied him. Even though he was unwell, no one was forcing him to marry and he had good kind friends to take care of him.

*

Inside the castle Rosanna could see from the top of the hill, William, the Earl of Melton, tossed restlessly in his bed under its deep blue silk canopy.

His dark hair was tangled over a face that was pale and drawn with pain.

George and Verity Blackwood stood at the side of his bed, gazing down in dismay.

"*Angel*, must find my *angel*," the Earl muttered in his delirium.

Lady Verity's thin lips pursed in disgust. "Why does he keep asking for an angel? Is he dying? Goodness, this is becoming intolerable, George."

She stared around the grand bedroom. The windows were tightly closed and the air was oppressive and unsavoury.

Viscount Blackwood looked uncomfortable and ashamed. He knew he should be doing more for his old friend, but had no idea what.

"I thought the waters at Bath would help, but he seems worse since our return," he said miserably.

"Perhaps our presence is hindering his recovery," Verity said slowly as a course of action suggested itself to her. "The strong feelings he has for me may make him worry about my seeing him in this fashion. No lady should be faced with such an unsavoury picture of her future husband."

George rubbed a fat hand over his face. Lord, he was hot and life at the castle was certainly not comfortable. The staff were only concerned with their sick master and even the meals had become hurried and dull.

To tell the truth he was bored and the thought of his rumbustious life back in London was very tempting.

"Do you think we should leave, sister?" he questioned, trying not to sound hopeful.

Verity pulled her cream lace shawl tighter around her deep mauve morning dress, as if to shut out the clammy air in the bedroom.

"Yes, George, I do. I think we should return to London immediately, leaving word to be sent for as soon as William has recovered."

The Viscount's better nature stirred for a second or two.

"Seems harsh to leave a friend alone like this. What will people say?"

Verity shrugged and walked out of the room without a backwards glance at the sick Earl.

"Anyone who is anyone will realise we are doing it with the very best of intentions. I am sure William will thank us when he regains his health. Come, George. I will inform the servants that they should pack our things immediately."

*

Rosanna trotted Taffy along the path back towards Donnington Hall. She was reluctant to return, but recognised that she must. No matter how she felt about Sir

Walter and the others, they were her guests and they had to be treated with a show of manners.

As the path crossed the road leading up to the Racecourse, she reined to a halt as a string of beautiful horses walked past.

The groom was a man of around thirty with brown hair and a tanned, good-natured face. He was riding the lead horse and touched his hat to her. "My Lady."

"Good morning. What marvellous horses. Who do they belong to?"

"Lord Melton, my Lady. I am his head groom, John Barker. My Master has permission to use the Racecourse to train his horses from Sir Leonard himself. I am taking them up there now for a training gallop."

Rosanna smiled. "I am Lady Rosanna Donnington. I own the Racecourse now, but of course you can continue to use it. How is your master? I believe he has been unwell."

John Barker frowned as the line of horses and their young grooms passed them by.

"He is still very sick, my Lady. He was thrown by his stallion and has not recovered from his injuries. We're all that worried about him."

Rosanna looked at him curiously. The groom sounded genuinely upset. 'The Earl must treat his staff very well,' she thought, 'for them to show such concern.'

"No doubt his doctors will do their very best to make his recovery a speedy one," she said.

The groom frowned. "Beggin' your pardon if I'm speaking out of turn, my Lady, but the doctor seems to leave it all to the nurses that he sends. And some of them seem to be no better than they should be."

"But the Earl's friends are in attendance, are they not?"

John Barker shook his head. "Their carriage was

setting out for London as I was leaving the stable yard this morning, my Lady. They've left my master on his own."

Rosanna frowned, but there was no more she could say on the subject.

She bade the groom good day and rode back to Donnington Hall, wondering how anyone who called themselves friends could be so unkind as to leave a sick man alone.

Then all thoughts of Lord Melton were banished from her head as she saw Sir Walter standing, waiting for her on the stone steps leading up to the front door.

She bit her lip. There was no way she could ride past him. She had to stop, but how dare he stand there, so arrogant, hands on hips, as if he were the owner and master of the house.

"Rosanna, my dearest, there you are!"

Sir Walter walked down the steps and held out his arms to catch her as she dismounted.

For a horrid second she could feel his hot breath on her cheek and his hands held her far too close to his chest.

He was not a tall man and his lips, which were red and wet, were only inches away from hers.

Rosanna controlled the shudder that ran through her body and pushed herself away from Sir Walter's grasp.

"I must go and change," she said. "I have had no breakfast yet. Have you eaten, Sir Walter?"

He frowned. "Well, your butler produced some sort of repast, but not of the amount and quality that Donnington Hall should offer their guests. When I am – "

He stopped but Rosanna could guess only too well what his next words would have been. '*When I am your husband and master of the house*!' She harboured no doubts about that.

"And will you be leaving today?" she asked as she handed Taffy's reins to a groom.

Sir Walter smiled. "Oh, no, my dear. Whatever put that quaint idea into your pretty little head. I intend to make myself quite indispensable here. Soon you will be wondering how you ever managed without me."

Rosanna did not reply. She ran up the steps, into the house, seeking the sanctuary of her own room.

She no longer felt hungry and she certainly could not face the thought of meeting the others in the breakfast room.

Swiftly she changed out of her riding habit into a pale green morning gown. The maid, Jenny, was useful but Rosanna wished with all her heart that Edie, her maid in London, was with her.

The little Cockney girl had a way of cheering her up that Rosanna found refreshing in a world of false behaviour and servile attendants.

When she walked downstairs, she met Bates in the hall.

"You have a visitor, my Lady," he announced.

"At this hour?"

"It is Mr. Howard who is on the Board of the local hospital," he replied.

"What can he want of me?"

Bates hesitated before saying,

"Well, Sir Leonard always helped the hospital because he said that people who were ill could not help themselves. I think that Mr. Howard is here to ask you to assist him in some fashion."

"Where have you put him?"

"In the study, my Lady."

Rosanna sighed, squared her shoulders and walked briskly down the corridor to the study.

It was no good shirking her responsibilities. If she could enjoy all the advantages of being an heiress, she had to accept that she had a role to play in local society as well.

When she entered the room, an elderly man with white hair turned from the window and approached her.

"Forgive me, Lady Rosanna, for calling on you so early in the morning," he began, "but I was afraid you might be returning to London and I was determined to see you before you left."

Rosanna shook his hand. "I have come here to stay," she said. "Now, how can I help you, Mr. Howard?"

"I represent the local hospital. Your late great-uncle was always most generous in his donations for its upkeep. At present we do not have enough nursing staff for our needs. We are situated so deep in the countryside here that girls do not want to come to work for us."

He sank into a chair and Rosanna sat opposite him, interested to listen to what he was saying.

"It is so hard to find experienced people. Why, even the Earl of Melton, who is well able to pay, is experiencing great difficulty in finding a nurse who will stay for more than a week."

"But if you paid better wages than in the towns, would not more girls come to the hospital?"

Mr. Howard nodded enthusiastically. "That is exactly the situation. And so I have come to you for a donation. I am quite desperate. Sir Leonard gave us, out of the kindness of his heart, five hundred pounds last year but without more, we may have to close the hospital. We have good doctors, but without the nurses, a hospital fails."

Rosanna reached out and placed a gentle hand on his arm. She could see that this elderly gentleman was, indeed, very distressed and worried about his patients.

"I am not certain how much I have in my bank account

at present," she said. "But I can certainly let you have two hundred pounds. When I know exactly how my income is managed, I will send you more."

Mr. Howard drew in a deep breath. Rosanna could see from the expression on his face just how much this meant to him.

"Why, thank you, Lady Rosanna," he said. "I cannot begin to tell you how grateful I am. It is horrifying for me to see patients being neglected or left uncomfortable because there is no one to attend to them."

Rosanna rose and Mr. Howard followed.

"I will send the necessary authority over to you at the hospital today," she said and rang the bell for Bates to show him out.

When he had departed, she sat at her uncle's wide desk, admiring the inlaid patterns on the top, fingering the beautiful blue Delft ink wells and tortoiseshell pens, and wrote out the necessary paperwork.

When she rang for Bates once more, she could tell by his expression that she had done the right thing.

She handed him the envelope and he nodded his appreciation.

"I will have your letter sent over to Mr. Howard straight away, my Lady," he said warmly. "And if I may make so bold as to say, Sir Leonard would have been delighted that you are continuing his charity work."

Rosanna sighed. "I have a feeling that this is only the first of many requests," she said. "I must form a clearer idea of my income before too many more applicants arrive on our doorstep."

She sat for a while on the window seat, gazing down at the manicured lawns and flower beds. A peacock was wandering across the grass, its long tail a gleaming cascade of blue and green.

How beautiful this house was and how lucky she was to own it.

She sighed, wondering how her father could have borne to have sold the house and estate to his uncle all those years ago. How marvellous it would have been to have grown up here. She could almost picture herself as a child, playing on that vast lawn, riding a fat little pony around the paddock.

Rosanna hoped and prayed that her dear parents and brother were watching from somewhere in Heaven, pleased that at last she was back where she belonged.

Suddenly she stiffened as she watched Sir Walter striding across the lawn, snapping some instructions to one of the gardeners.

How dare he act as if he owned the place! She felt a shiver of real fear cross her mind. He was not the type of man who would go away just because she asked him. He was determined to marry her and, at present, she could not see a way of defeating him.

She had run away once and he had found her. But on reflection, her destination had been quite obvious.

The beginning of a new idea began to form – perhaps next time she would run somewhere he would never think of looking!

CHAPTER FOUR

Rosanna spent half an hour in the kitchens, discussing the day's menus with Mrs. Bates, who was still worried about providing meals for so many at such short notice.

"I'm sure I hope we'll cope, my Lady," she said eventually. "Supplies are being sent from the town and we have plenty of our own fruit and vegetables, of course. It's just the special things the guests ask for which might be difficult to provide. And, of course, Sir Leonard did not keep a very extensive cellar. Sir Walter and the other gentlemen have already drunk several bottles of wine and brandy."

Rosanna tossed back her long blonde hair that kept escaping its bonds.

"Just do your best, Mrs. Bates. I ask for no more," she said. "I am hoping that they will soon be on their way home to London!"

When she left the kitchen, she was crossing the hall when Sir Walter appeared.

"I hope you will be making plans to return to London soon, sir."

Because she had been thinking it, the words seemed to slip from her lips. Then to her astonishment and distress, Sir Walter came very close and placed his hands on her shoulders.

"Now listen to me, my darling," he said. "You are

43

going to marry me and the sooner we do so, the better. I love you and I know you love me. I am thrilled with Donnington Hall and would suggest we live here, as I am sure we would be happier than in my own home which is more of a bachelor residence."

He paused for breath before he hurried on to say,

"I can see us giving marvellous parties and together we will take our position as the leaders of Society in the county."

As he finished speaking, he drew her closer to him and bent forward to kiss her.

His lips were seeking hers but somehow, in disgust, Rosanna managed to turn her head so that he kissed, not her lips, but her cheek.

She tried to pull away, but his big hands only held her tighter.

"Sir, please, your friends could be here at any second," she gasped.

"I agree they are a nuisance," Sir Walter answered. "But the girls are a necessity as chaperones. I will tell them to go back to London as soon as you and I can be married in the local church. I shall seek out the Vicar as soon as possible. Presumably there will be certain legal documents that need to be attended to, but most of these country clergy are very amenable to a few guineas in their pockets."

He paused before he continued,

"We might travel over to Paris for a short honeymoon before we start training the best and the fastest of the horses in your stables on the Racecourse which your uncle built so brilliantly."

Rosanna stared into his face. Suddenly his eyes were gleaming in a way they had not when he had been speaking about marriage and she could hear the enthusiasm in his voice when he discussed racing. He was obviously fanatical about the sport.

She had heard of men who gave their whole lives to racing horses and gambling and she realised that Sir Walter was just such a person.

Her spirits sank even lower. How could she fight against an obsession such as this? He would in some way force her to marry him so he could get his hands on not just her money and estate, but the Racecourse and the horses.

She held everything he wanted, and that was not herself, but what she possessed.

'Help me, God. Please help me,' she prayed. At the same time, she was pushing Sir Walter away. But he only released her when there was the sound of approaching voices.

"I want to be alone with you," he whispered, his lips hot and wet against her ear. "I want to tell you how happy we will be together and to plan our marriage."

As Susan and Miranda descended the great stairway, Rosanna pulled away from Sir Walter and ran past them without speaking.

She could hear the odious man laughing and the words, " – embarrassed by you seeing our love for each other."

Oh, this was intolerable. She had to escape. She had no choice but to run away again.

The housemaids were working in her bedroom, so she hurried further along the corridor and up a flight of stairs to a small room Bates had shown her on her tour of the house.

It had been where the nurse had slept who had cared for the late Sir Leonard during the few short days of his final illness.

Rosanna recalled absentmindedly opening and

shutting drawers in the dressing table and seeing a few objects left behind by mistake.

She had paid no particular notice at the time, but now –

Yes! There they were. A nurse's uniform – plain grey dress, long white apron, clean and pressed, a white cap, a notebook containing a list of her previous patients.

There was also a belt with a fancy buckle and a little bunch of scissors and measuring spoons, wrapped in soft leather. They were exactly what she wanted.

She remembered with a pang how carefully she had watched Nurse Evans who had cared for her dear mother during her last illness. They had spoken many times and Rosanna had often taken over some of the arduous tasks whilst the nurse was sleeping.

Nurse Evans had given her much information about her profession. If her plan was to work, she would need to remember everything in great detail.

Returning to her room, Rosanna hurriedly packed a small case with her plainest clothes and washing utensils. She only took a silver backed hair brush, but hopefully nobody would see it.

She pushed the case under her bed and slipped downstairs again. The house was very quiet. Obviously Sir Walter and the others had gone into the garden. Thank goodness. Luck was on her side at last.

She went to find her butler.

"Bates, I need to go out," she said. "I want to go alone and not be bothered by any of my guests. While I change my clothes, will you fetch one of the horses and prevent anyone from coming with me?"

"That will be a difficult task, my Lady," Bates said frowning.

"I know," Rosanna replied. "But hopefully you can manage it, dear Bates."

"Will you ride the mare Taffy, my Lady?"

Rosanna sighed. Even in the short time she had been at Donnington Hall, she had grown to love the beautiful mare, but knew it was not the type of mount she needed at this moment.

"No, not this time. I noticed a rather plain, plump grey pony in the stables. I believe his name is Smudger. If he could be saddled and left at the end of the little lane leading out across the fields, that would be extremely helpful.

"Then I need you to find Henry, my coachman, and tell him to take the carriage and drive back to the London house immediately."

Bates looked anxious. "May I ask where you are heading, my Lady? Although this is a gentle area, there are always ruffians around."

"There is more danger for me here, Bates," Rosanna responded solemnly. "I do not need to tell you what. I am sure it is obvious. I want to get rid of them, but you know it is very difficult for me. You are being so kind and understanding that I can only say how grateful I am both to you and to your wife for your support."

"We've had worse things than this to conquer," Bates said with a grim smile.

"What you must tell my guests, including Sir Walter, is that I have a friend in the North of the country who is extremely ill and likely to die. I have therefore gone to see her as quickly as I could."

She smiled at him as she added, "you can say that I have suggested that they all go back to London."

There was silence for a moment before Bates said,

"I expect Sir Walter will ask me details about your friend."

"You can tell him the truth," Rosanna answered. "You can say you only know that she lives somewhere in the North, Yorkshire perhaps, and as I was in such a hurry I did not give you the address. Hopefully he will see that the carriage has gone and think it is carrying me northwards."

"I will do my best, my Lady, but you know what Sir Walter is like. He goes on and on until he gets what he wants, as far as I can see."

"I know that," Rosanna replied. "That is why I need to go away. And quickly. I dare not stop here. I cannot fight him at present. He is too strong."

"How will your Ladyship know when to return if I cannot contact you?"

Rosanna frowned as an idea came to her. "On the roof there are several flags, Bates. I saw them when I was exploring. When the visitors have finally left, fly a flag from the flagpole and I will know my home is my own again."

"So you will not be going far, my Lady?"

Rosanna just smiled.

"Well, if your Ladyship doesn't want them to know where you are going, I will have the pony ready for you in a quarter of an hour."

"Thank you! Thank you!" Rosanna cried.

Bates nodded gravely and watched as the slim figure sped back up the stairway. He sighed and went to give orders to Henry about the carriage and to the groom to saddle the pony.

He led the animal down the little back lane to where the fields began and tethered him to a post.

Slipping behind some thick bushes, he watched in amazement as a few minutes later what appeared to be a young nurse wearing a severe dress in grey and a dark cloak, hurried down the path, fastened her case to the pony's saddle, mounted and trotted away across the fields.

Once she was out in the open country, Rosanna gave the pony its head and rode as quickly as she could.

It was some distance to the Earl of Melton's castle, but she knew exactly where it was from her earlier ride.

She stopped at a little stream and let Smudger take a drink. She patted his warm neck. It seemed strange to be riding a pony after the lovely Taffy, but an ordinary nurse would not have access to a thoroughbred mare.

Twenty minutes later, Rosanna walked the pony out of a field through a gate into a road lined on either side with great chestnut trees.

She slipped off the pony and led it under the bright green shade to the castle gates.

To her surprise they were not closed and there was no sign of the gatekeeper.

'Oh, no,' Rosanna murmured. 'This is an obvious indication that their master is sick and not in control of his affairs. I am sure that such slackness would not have happened if he had been in good health.'

She pushed the gates wider, led Smudger through, then sprang into the saddle and trotted up the long drive towards the castle.

Rosanna reined the pony to a halt and let it crop some grass while she studied the magnificent building before her. Much older than Donnington Hall, it was a perfect small castle, right down to the battlements and the drawbridge across the moat that lead under an ancient gateway into the forecourt.

But for all its beauty, it had a forlorn look. There was thick green slime on the surface of the moat and the windows looked dingy.

'Please God this will be my chance to escape,' she thought. 'It is the only ruse I can think of. It must succeed!'

Rosanna walked across the bridge into the castle grounds and ignoring the heavy studded front door, she took her mount to the stable yard. A man who was cleaning a carriage, looked around at her in surprise.

"Good morning, I have come to see his Lordship," she announced, stepping forward gingerly over the puddles on the cobblestones, "and I think it would be best for me to leave my pony with you rather than outside the front door."

"It'll certainly be safer," the man replied with a grin.

"That is what I thought," Rosanna replied. "He is very good and perhaps you would be kind enough to give him a drink and a rub down as it is very hot and we have ridden a long way."

"I'll do that, don't you worry, miss," the man said.

He did not seem curious as to why she was at the castle, which gave Rosanna hope. Obviously nurses were an expected sight these days, so none of the staff would be likely to gossip about her in the village.

Rosanna hesitated as she left the stable yard. She was not at all sure if she should go round to the main door of the castle, but decided that it would be more diplomatic to knock at the staff entrance and enquire.

There was quite a pause before the door was opened by a footman, who asked her to come inside and went to summon the butler. An elderly man with white hair finally appeared.

"Can I help you, miss?"

"I wonder if I might see his Lordship," Rosanna asked. "My name is Nurse – Nurse Robinson." She stumbled over the name, giving her maid, Edie's, surname as it was the only one that came readily to her mind.

"I understand the Earl is very anxious to hire a nurse and as I am staying in the neighbourhood, I thought I might come and enquire."

The elderly man stared at her. "So you are a nurse?" he asked.

"I have been for a number of years," Rosanna told him, "and have done very well. But I am bored with working in towns and would like to live in the country."

"Most people who come here say the opposite," the butler replied. "But I am sure his Lordship will be pleased to see you."

"That is what I hoped," Rosanna responded with a smile.

"Then please come this way," the butler said.

She followed him down a long stone passage into the main part of the castle. A huge marble floored hall lay before her, where ancestral flags hung from poles and sumptuous heavy tapestries covered the walls.

Deep copper bowls of flowers sat on heavy oak chests, highlighted in ruby and emerald by the rays of sunlight that flooded down through the stained glass in the side windows.

But Rosanna noticed that most of the flowers had faded and the water needed changing in the bowls.

The butler led her up a steep flight of stairs that curved round and round until they reached the first landing.

"If you would care to wait a moment, miss, I will check that it is convenient for his Lordship to see you."

Rosanna nodded and grasped her bag nervously between her hands. The nurse's uniform felt stiff and strange to her, but in some way it seemed easier to act this part wearing a costume.

The door opened and the butler said, "will you come in, miss. His Lordship will be pleased to see you."

Rosanna walked into what she thought could have been a very attractive apartment. It was high-ceilinged with good proportions, but the deep windows at one side were shut and curtained, making the room dark and gloomy.

The air was oppressive and far too warm. In the centre of the room stood a large four-poster bed draped with blue silk curtains that were heavily embroidered in gold thread with the Melton coat of arms.

The same coat of arms was embroidered above the untidy pile of pillows. Sitting up in bed was the owner, William, the Earl of Melton.

Rosanna stared at him. Yes, this was the invalid she had seen at the inn the other day. As she remembered, he was a handsome man, not a day over thirty, but his face was pale and ravaged by pain, his thick dark hair unbrushed and lying unruly over his forehead. He badly needed a shave and his hands were restless on top of the sheets.

"Good morning, nurse," he said wearily. "I understand you wish to see me."

He held out his hand and Rosanna walked to the side of the bed and shook it.

She was aware of long fingers that clasped hers weakly and then fell away. She sat on a chair which had obviously been arranged for her.

"I asked to see your Lordship," Rosanna began, "because I have been told you have need of a live-in nurse. In fact, I was told you do not have one here in the house at present, which would be convenient, but that you have to send to the hospital every day for one to come to you."

"That is true," the Earl answered, "and they never stop telling me what a nuisance I am."

He laughed a little bitterly as he spoke.

"It must be upsetting for you as well as for them," Rosanna said. "Well, as I am a nurse and like the countryside, I thought I might be useful to you."

"Are you really a nurse?" the Earl asked. "It is dark in here and you sound very young."

"I have been a nurse for several years," she told him. "I have my qualifications and references, but as I am on holiday, I am afraid they are in London and it will take a little time to bring them to you."

"If you are free now and are prepared to give up your time," the Earl enquired, "could you come to me at once?"

"That is what I would like," Rosanna responded, "because where I am staying is overcrowded and I am quite certain I would find your house restful. I promise you that I can bandage your leg as well as any local nurse would be able to do."

"That is the best news I have heard for years," the Earl said. "When they can spare a nurse from the hospital one arrives, but they never fail to point out that I am preventing them attending to people who are far worse than I am."

He tossed restlessly in the bed. "And, of course, they are right. This stupid injury and fever will not improve. Sometimes – " he shot a glance at Rosanna through thickly lashed eyes – "I doubt if I will ever recover."

Rosanna stood up and began to straighten the bedclothes.

"That, if you will pardon my saying so, my Lord, is just the fever speaking. With a little rest and care, I am sure you will be up and about in no time."

"I envy you your confidence, Nurse Robinson. I only wish I shared it. Well, Digby will show you your room," the Earl said lying back, exhausted. "I must try to sleep."

She watched as he drifted off into an uneasy doze and then turned to find Mr. Digby, the butler, standing waiting for her in the gloom.

"He seems very weak," she whispered.

Mr. Digby nodded. "He is indeed, miss. No strength in him at all. He won't eat, although cook has prepared some nourishing broths. Very upsetting it is to see the Master laid so low."

Behind them, the Earl began to mutter.

"*Angel* – oh, *angel*, why don't you come to me?"

Rosanna bit her lip and allowed the butler to show her to her room. Obviously there was someone in the Earl's life who would do him some good. Perhaps it would be in her power to find her and bring him some joy.

*

Later that evening, a little shabby figure could be seen walking slowly up the long driveway towards Donnington Hall.

Edie Robinson had just alighted from the coach down in the village. She had been travelling all day from London and was exhausted.

'Come on, Edie, pick your feet up smartish or my Lady will be wondering where you're at,' she said to herself, scowling apprehensively at a little group of black and white cows who were grazing nearby.

She changed her heavy tapestry carry bag from one hand to the other so she could hit them if they came any closer.

'Cor, fine old place this is,' she muttered, staring up at the impressive outline of the Hall. 'Fancy Lady Rosanna owning all this. Wouldn't like to be a housemaid here. How about lugging coal up to those bedrooms! And bringing the ashes down again!'

Edie had been Rosanna's maid for two years now. At eighteen, but small for her age, she was very thin, with a halo of bright red curls which she forced under control by wearing her maid's hat pulled down tightly onto her forehead.

She had begun work with the Donningtons as a housemaid, but Rosanna and her mother had been taken by the young Cockney girl's quickness and ability to get things done and promoted her to be Rosanna's own personal maid.

It had been unfortunate that Edie had been away visiting her family in the East End of London when Rosanna fled to Donnington Hall. She had followed as fast as she could, but had no idea of why her Mistress had left town so speedily.

Edie made her way round to the back of the house and knocked on the servants' door.

The butler, Bates, was summoned and she was ushered into the kitchen.

'Your Mistress is not here at present," Bates told her. "I am not sure when she will return."

"Well, that's a turn up," Edie replied taking a large mouthful of the piece of cake the cook had offered her. "Where has she gone?"

"Well, the county of Yorkshire was mentioned," Bates said, gazing around him in an uneasy fashion, as if he was scared of being overheard.

Edie stared at him, sensing that something was not quite right, but realising he was not going to tell her anything further just at present.

"What do you think I should do then, Mr. Bates?"

The butler hesitated.

"I imagine it would be best if you perhaps helped with the sewing and laundry until my Lady returns."

"Righty ho!" Edie stood up and hoisted her bag into her arms. "If someone could just show me where to leave me bag, I'll get started."

The maid Jenny who had been looking after Rosanna until Edie arrived was called and escorted the London girl upstairs.

"She's lovely, your Mistress," she said as they climbed the steep back stairs to the attic rooms. "You're very lucky being her maid."

"Don't I know it," Edie said brightly. "And this is a lovely old house. Do you like working here?"

Jenny frowned. "It was very quiet when old Sir Leonard was alive. But things have got a bit livelier lately and that's a fact."

Just as they reached the top corridor, a door opened and a man strode out. Broad shouldered and red faced, he looked very angry.

The two girls flattened themselves against the wall as he flung open another door, peered inside and then slammed the door shut again.

Suddenly he spotted the maids. "You, girl, who are you? I don't recognise your face."

Edie bobbed a little curtsy to him. She knew very well who this was – Sir Walter Fenwick.

"Edie Robinson, Sir. I'm Lady Rosanna's maid, come down from London."

"And do you know where your Mistress is, Edie? I reckon she has told you where to meet her, eh?"

Edie looked up at him, puzzled. "No, sir, I've no idea."

Sir Walter plucked a small coin out of his pocket and held it in front of her eyes.

"Here, my dear. Perhaps this will jog your memory!"

Edie stiffened. She had heard a lot of gossip about Sir Walter and was surprised to find him here. But Edie was older than her years. She had a very good idea that Sir Walter had smelled the money that her Mistress now possessed and wanted a part of it.

"I'm sorry, Sir, I dunno where Lady Rosanna is," she said, putting on her most simple expression.

Sir Walter's face darkened down to a fine shade of maroon.

"Well, wherever she is, she obviously doesn't need your attentions. You can go. Get out. Here's half a sovereign. That should pay your wages for the month. You are dismissed."

Edie was stunned. "But where shall I go, sir?"

Sir Walter waved her away as if she was an annoying insect.

"Just get out of sight," he snapped. "Go back to London. Go anywhere. You are no longer in service to Lady Rosanna Donnington."

CHAPTER FIVE

The next day, late morning shadows were casting patterns across the great courtyard of Melton Castle. The air was very still. There was the taste of thunder in the air and on the far horizon, towards Donnington Hall, great black and purple clouds boiled in the sky.

Rosanna had slipped down to the stables to check that her pony had been well cared for.

The nurse's dark grey uniform still felt odd and she had no idea how her gold hair gleamed against the subdued colour, even under the hideous cap she had struggled to pin firmly on her head.

The Earl had been sleeping that morning when she had enquired if she was needed. She found this worrying. Should he sleep so much? Surely if his health was improving, he should be out of bed by now?

He had not sent for Rosanna the evening before and she had lain in the hard, narrow bed in her little room, wondering what was happening back at Donnington Hall.

How had Sir Walter reacted to her disappearance? Poor Bates would have had to bear the brunt of his displeasure.

Breakfast had been an adequate meal, served in the big kitchen. She had sat silently near the head of the table, only speaking when spoken to.

She was well aware that her accent was different to that of the other staff, but hoped they would think she was a gentlewoman who had fallen on hard times.

Luckily, Mr. Digby ran below stairs with a rod of iron. He was old-fashioned in his ways and did not approve of chatter at the meal tables.

In a way it was a relief not to have to act the nurse right away, but she knew she would soon have to change the bandages on the Earl's leg as they had not been touched for days.

'My goodness,' she gasped now as she entered the main stable block. Row upon row of beautiful horses stared back from their loose boxes.

'I had no idea the Earl owned so many. No wonder his father and my great-uncle got on so well. How I would love to ride some of these beauties.'

Rosanna moved down the centre aisle, stopping now and then to pat an inquisitive head or rub a velvety nose that stretched towards her.

She found one stall with the name '*Demon*' on a sign above it. Inside was a great black stallion and she knew this was the animal the Earl had been riding when he had suffered his dreadful accident.

Demon turned to face her, but Rosanna felt no fear. She picked up a piece of discarded apple from the floor and, with it flat on the palm of her hand, held it out towards the stallion.

For a long minute he just stared at her and then something in her manner must have pleased him, because he deigned to take the apple and allowed her to respectfully rub the space between his eyes until he tossed his head and backed away.

Rosanna smiled. "All right, your Majesty," she said fondly. "I will not presume on your dignity any longer."

She found her pony, Smudger, well stabled at the far end. He was wearing a rug and had been fed and watered.

Rosanna was pleased to see that just because he belonged to the nurse, he was not treated any differently to the thoroughbreds that surrounded him.

She fondled his rough mane and whispered, 'oh, Smudger, let us hope we will both soon be back where we belong.'

As she turned to go, she heard voices and stepped back into the shelter of the pony's stall. At present she did not want to explain her presence to anyone else.

All servants tended to gossip and the least number of people who knew that the nurse living at the castle was interested in horses, the better. Such news could get back to Sir Walter very quickly.

She was glad she had taken refuge as a few seconds later, John Barker, the head groom she had met when he was exercising the Earl's racehorses, passed the stall entrance, talking to another man.

Rosanna bit her lip and pressed herself closer to the wooden sides of the stall. The haynet tickled her nose, but she was determined not to sneeze.

This was someone she had to avoid for as long as possible. John Barker would know exactly who she was. The nurse's uniform would not fool him.

When they had gone, she fled back to the castle. She thought she heard him call after her, but told herself he was too far away to have seen her face.

Calming herself, she made her way up to her room to fetch her nurse's bag, before hurrying down the curving stairway to the Earl's bedroom.

A young man with blond hair, wearing a valet's uniform in the dark blue Melton colours, was standing outside the door, about to enter. He looked round as Rosanna approached.

"Oh, hello. You must be the new nurse. I missed you at breakfast. I was on duty up here. I am Peter Simkins, his Lordship's valet."

Rosanna had the presence of mind to hold out her hand. She must remember that here in the castle she was a servant, an upper class servant to be sure, but still not one of the gentry as she would be at home.

"Good morning, Mr. Simkins. I am Nurse Robinson. Pleased to make your acquaintance. Are you about to attend to the Earl?"

Simkins nodded gloomily. "And in a rare bad mood he's in, too. He's already thrown a cup and saucer at me."

Rosanna felt her heart sink. "Perhaps his injuries are paining him badly?" she ventured.

"Something's irritated him and no mistake. Can I get you anything, nurse?"

Rosanna thought for a second and answered firmly, "yes, a bowl of fresh warm water and some soft clean cloths, please."

The young man nodded and walked away, obviously glad not to have to face his Master at this moment.

Rosanna took a deep breath, turned the handle and walked in. This was going to be so difficult and so dangerous. Her very first chance to make the Earl believe she really was a nurse.

As she entered, the oppressive gloom of the room swept over her once more. Instinctively, she ran to the windows, flung back the heavy blue brocade curtains and thrust open one of the casements.

The air that rushed in was warm, but smelled sweet, carrying a hint of rain and roses on it.

"That smells wonderful," the Earl's voice broke the

silence.

Rosanna turned and smiled. He was sitting up in bed, leaning on his pillows. His lawn nightshirt was open at the neck and she could see the gleam of sweat on his throat. His dark hair was tousled and he still badly needed a shave.

"I know the fashionable idea is to shut out all chances of catching a chill, but I think a little fresh air helps a patient to recover," she stated sedately, trying to remember how Nurse Evans, her mother's nurse, had spoken.

"Recovery seems a long way off with this wretched leg," the Earl snarled. "I feel so damned weak all the time. Some mornings I seem a little better, then by the evening, I am exhausted again. Ridiculous! I just want to be strong enough to ride again."

Rosanna felt a surge of pity sweep through her. Lying there, he reminded her of a great injured beast, a lion or a tiger, all that strength diminished, lashing out in anger at his own incapacitated state.

She was sure that much of his failure to recover was caused by the frustration boiling through his veins. A man such as William, the Earl of Melton, would never rest easily in his bed and give his wounds time to heal.

Just then a knock at the door heralded Peter Simkins with the bowl of water. He placed it on a small table and, without further words, turned back the sheets and blankets from the foot of the bed to reveal his master's feet and lower limbs.

Rosanna felt a rosy flush begin to stain her cheeks. She fought to control it. This was dreadful. There was no way a nurse would blush at the sight of a gentleman's legs!

She realised that this was the reality of her dilemma. In theory when she had run away, pretending to be a nurse, it had seemed like an easy way out. She was convinced that she could manage. She was sure she had the right skills to tend a wound and bandage and care for a patient.

But now she had to admit that actually physically attending to a man had never featured in her imagination.

"Well, don't just stand there, Nurse Robinson. Remove this wretched bandage and tell me what you think."

Taking a deep breath, Rosanna walked calmly up to the bed and selecting her sharpest scissors, snipped away the thick bandage that covered the Earl's left leg from just below the knee down to his ankle.

As the covering fell away and revealed the wound, Rosanna realised that the valet, who was standing on the other side of the bed, had gone very pale.

He was staring down at the jagged flesh and with a muttered apology, rushed out of the room, one hand clapped to his mouth.

The Earl grunted. "Simkins has a weak stomach," he admitted dryly. "I hope you don't mind being alone in the room with me, nurse?"

Rosanna looked up and smiled. "Not while I have these scissors in my hand, my Lord!"

The Earl began to laugh, then stopped and flinched. He lay and watched as the young nurse began to bathe his leg. Her touch was so gentle, it hardly hurt at all.

"Indeed, that does feel a great deal better," he said at last.

Rosanna picked up the clean bandages and then hesitated.

"If I may make so bold as to say, my Lord," she said, "I have known other cases where exposure to the fresh air helped the healing process."

The Earl glared but nodded. "Well, nurse, it cannot get any worse."

"I would suggest that just for an hour or maybe two,

we leave your leg unbandaged."

"And do you have any schemes up your capable sleeve to rid me of this fever and lethargy?" he asked, lying back against the pillows as the weariness overcame him once more.

Rosanna gazed down at him. How broad his shoulders seemed inside his nightshirt. And although his leg was badly damaged, she had seen that it was heavily muscled as well. She could imagine quite clearly what a fine figure he would cut on horseback.

But she could also see that his face was that of a kind, good natured man. There was none of the dissolution and marks of heavy drinking that marred Sir Walter's countenance.

"I am sure that your staff have been preparing small wholesome meals for you – " she began tactfully.

"What! That damn slop Simkins and Digby bring me. It's enough to turn a man's stomach!"

Rosanna sighed. She had been fairly certain in her own mind that most of the Earl's troubles were caused by neglect. His valet seemed too young and inexperienced and Mr. Digby was too old.

She wished she could send for Bates and Mrs. Bates from Donnington Hall. Their care would soon bring the Earl back to good health, she was sure.

"Have you no friends or family you could call on to stand by you at this time, my Lord?" she ventured, hoping she would not be thought insolent for making such a remark.

The Earl's dark brows drew together in a thunderous glare.

"I thought – two great friends of mine were here when the accident occurred. Indeed, they took the trouble to have me transported to Bath to see if the waters would help. But nothing worked and my friends have now returned to

London."

Rosanna said nothing, busying herself in tidying away her equipment and making the room look as pleasant as possible.

She wondered if it was the female friend whom the Earl had called his '*angel*', when speaking in his delirium earlier.

As she turned to leave the room, she said quietly,

"One of the most important things about being ill is that you must make yourself believe, through your mind and your will, that you are going to get well quickly."

The Earl stared at her. This nurse was so very different from the others who had attended him in the last few weeks.

He thought she seemed a strange girl. He wished he could see her hair clearly – it was covered by the awful cap she wore, but what he could spy was bright golden.

He did notice that she was tall and slender and that her grey uniform was too big for her.

He wondered if she, too, had been ill recently. She seemed to impart a deep well of compassion that he had not experienced in nurses before.

As he looked closely, he could see that there were, indeed, dark shadows under her eyes which were a brilliant blue.

"Where are you going now?" he asked impulsively, not wanting her to leave.

Rosanna smiled. "Down to the kitchen, my Lord," she said firmly. "I will oversee your lunch today and I am quite sure it will be something you will enjoy eating."

And with a swirl of her grey skirts, she left the room and to the Earl it seemed to grow darker with her going.

*

Far beneath them on the other side of the castle, a

65

small, red-headed girl was making her way slowly and wearily across the wooden ramp that led from the paddocks, across the moat and into the castle stable yard by way of a doorway wide enough to take the biggest carriages.

Although Sir Walter Fenwick had dismissed her, Edie still considered herself to be Lady Rosanna's maid. Until her Mistress told her in person that her services were no longer required, she would do her best to find her and report for duty.

"If the 'orrible Sir Walter finks he can buy me orf with 'alf a guinea, he's very much mistaken!" Edie said out loud, her Cockney accent becoming more pronounced because she was so annoyed.

She had spent the night sleeping in the maid Jenny's room.

She did not believe Lady Rosanna had gone to Yorkshire. As far as Edie knew, her Mistress knew no one in that county.

As she had left Donnington Hall that morning, Bates, the butler, had called her to one side and, with a worried glance over his shoulder to check no one was watching, pushed a little slip of paper into her hand.

Edie had waited until she was out of sight of the Hall before reading it.

She had the oddest feeling that she was being watched as she walked away up the long drive.

Once she spun round and could have sworn that Sir Walter was spying on her from one of the upstairs windows. Perhaps he thought she would head straight for Lady Rosanna.

The message from Bates read, "*Our Mistress might be at Melton Castle. But not as you know her. Take great care.*"

Edie read it three times but could not understand it any

better on the third attempt.

'Well, Melton Castle it is, then,' she muttered. 'I'll sort out the rest of the riddle when I get there.'

A long walk across country had brought her to the rear of the castle. She was aching for a nice cup of tea and the chance to take off her shoes which were pinching cruelly.

Just as she reached the wooden ramp that bridged the moat at that point, a flash of white and blue caught her eye. Edie glanced down at the muddy water and gasped.

The stone walls of the outer moat had crumbled at some point over the centuries and a muddy slope led down to the water.

A little girl in a blue dress and white pinafore was crouched down in the mud, pushing bits of twig and leaves into the water.

"Oi! Watch out! That looks deep there."

But even as Edie shouted, the child reached out too far, slipped and fell into the moat with a resounding splash.

The next few seconds were a whirl afterwards in Edie's brain. She remembered dropping her bag, kicking off her shoes and sliding down into the water.

She tangled her hands in the little girl's apron and tugged her up out of the water, but the weeds in the moat were already twining around her legs, trying to pull her down.

She heard a man shouting, the child screaming and then strong arms were round them both, hauling them up the side of the moat to the safety of the castle yard.

Coughing and spluttering, Edie scrambled to her feet. She was soaked to the waist but the little girl had gone right under and was crying, cold and shaking.

"Millie! Millie! You naughty girl. Look at you. Oh, thank you, miss. I only turned my head for a second and she was in the water."

"That's all right. Only glad I came along. But she needs to be dried quickly and found clean clothes."

The man had a tanned face and bright brown eyes. He grinned at the redhead.

"So do you, miss, if you don't mind me saying so. Come with me. I will look after my daughter and I've still got some of my late wife's garments stored away. If you don't mind wearing them, that is?"

Edie nodded. So he was a widower. And bringing up a child on his own. That was unusual. Most men she knew would have passed the child on to their mother or sister or remarried as quickly as they could.

Dripping, she picked up her bag and followed the man across the stable yard and into a snug little cottage. He ushered her into the kitchen where the range was warming the room.

Edie kicked off her shoes which she felt were past saving and stood shivering as the man hurried upstairs with the child. In a few moments he was back down, offering her a bundle of clothes.

He closed the door behind him and Edie grinned as she threw off the soaking garments, right down to her bodice and drawers. The dress fitted her well. Obviously the man's wife had been about the same size.

'Good job, too,' Edie muttered, rubbing her red curls with a towel. 'Been a bit of a laugh if the poor lady had been sixteen stone or so.'

She found a clean apron and her best shoes in her carry bag and felt a little more respectable.

While waiting, she busied herself in the kitchen. Although it was tidy, she put the kettle on the hob to boil and found some cups.

At long last the door opened and the man appeared.

"I've put Millie to bed. She's in disgrace," he said gravely. "She's been told over and over not to go near the water. Thank God you were passing. I can never thank you enough. Are you dry and warm now? I am John Barker, head groom to Lord Melton. You've already met my daughter, Millie!"

"Edie Robinson." Edie held out her hand and he shook it, frowning. "Personal maid to Lady Rosanna Donnington of Donnington Hall."

John Barker looked surprised. "That's odd. The new nurse who's come to look after the Earl is called Robinson, too. But why would you be seeking Lady Rosanna here at Melton Castle, Edie?"

Edie gasped. This was too big a coincidence. The 'nurse' must surely be Lady Rosanna. No wonder Mr. Bates had written '*but not as you know her*' in his note.

Her thoughts squirreled around in her head. What should she do?

There was no way she could just turn up at the castle door and ask for Lady Rosanna. Obviously her Mistress had not told anyone who she was and Edie's arrival could give the game away completely.

John Barker was taking bread and cheese from a cupboard and setting two places at the white scrubbed wooden table.

"You seem worried, Miss Robinson," he said. "Can I help in any way? I owe you so much today. I would do anything in my power to repay you."

Edie turned away and made the tea. She said nothing until they were seated, facing each other. "It's not my secret to tell, Mr. Barker."

"John, please! I think the time has passed for politeness."

"John. Can I trust you?"

He reached a broad tanned hand across the table and pressed her fingers briefly.

"Say nothing, but let me make a guess or two. The new nurse arrived unexpectedly at the castle, riding a rough moorland pony – which is a very strange way to take up a new employment. She only carried a small bag with her, according to the lad who first met her."

He took a large gulp of tea and continued, "she gave particular instructions on caring for the pony. So she obviously knows a great deal about horses – again not many nurses would do that.

"I've only seen her from a distance, myself, but Peter Simkins, my Master's valet, tells me she has the whitest and softest hands he has ever seen on a servant."

Edie smiled. She had a feeling that she did not need to break any confidences here. John Barker had guessed exactly who 'Nurse Robinson' was!

"What should I do?" she asked, enjoying the newly baked bread and creamy cheese and realising it was hours since she had eaten.

"If you stay here in my cottage there'll be gossip," John said.

Edie nodded, she knew how quickly a girl's reputation could vanish.

"That's true, but I need to be here at the castle in case my Mistress needs me. I cannot go back to London while she is in difficulties."

"Aye. That's true enough, lass. Listen, there's a little room at the back of the stables that I use to keep all the records of Lord Melton's racehorses. No one goes there but me. It's snug and dry and we could make up a bed on the floor. There's a privy just outside the stables.

"I'll tell the other lads that you are a cousin of my late wife who's fallen on hard times and are staying a few days on your way to London."

Edie's eyes sparkled. This was an adventure indeed. And she had thought life in the country would be boring!

*

That night the storm that had been threatening all day, finally broke. Great claps of thunder echoed around Melton Castle. White flashes of lightning pierced the curtains covering Rosanna's windows and the wind of the summer storm hurled itself against the ancient stones.

At around three in the morning, a particular vicious flash of lightning and peel of thunder brought Rosanna out of bed.

She lit the oil lamp on her dressing table and wrapping herself in her old dressing gown, pattered barefooted across the room to peer out of the window at the tossing trees and racing clouds.

The wind hurled rain against the glass until the panes shuddered in their frames.

'Nature can be so overwhelming in her force,' Rosanna murmured. 'I do hope my poor horses are being cared for back at Donnington Hall. They are so highly strung and will be scared by all this noise. I would not credit Sir Walter with knowing what to do in an emergency.'

She jumped violently as a knock came on her door. "Yes, who is it?" she called warily.

"Nurse Robinson – can you come – urgently."

Picking up the lamp, Rosanna hurried to the door and flung it wide. Peter Simkins stood outside, a candle in his hand, the flickering light reflecting on his worried face.

"I am so sorry to disturb you, nurse, but can you come to my Master."

Rosanna's heart beat faster.

"Is he worse?"

Peter nodded. "The fever is very high once again, nurse, and I rightly don't know what else to do for him."

"Wait – I will get dressed."

She whirled away, fear pounding through her. Had her lack of nursing ability caused this relapse? Had she done something dreadfully, terribly wrong to that splendid man?

She was stopped in her tracks by Peter's voice. "Please, nurse, come now. There isn't any time to lose. I think – I think the Earl might be going to die!"

CHAPTER SIX

Rosanna's bare feet made no sound as she hurried along the corridor and down the staircase to the great bedroom where the Earl lay.

The light from the oil lamp she carried threw weird shadows everywhere and it seemed to her as if the very stones of the old castle stirred sensing that danger surrounded their Master.

Candles were flickering wildly inside the Earl's room. The curtains were still open and the wind rattled the windows violently as the storm hit the castle over and over again.

Rosanna hurried to the bedside, aware that Peter was standing in the doorway. She had seen the panic in the valet's eyes and feared he would be of very little help.

The Earl was tossing and turning, sweat was wet on his face, his dark hair lank and damp. Rosanna bent over him and touched his cheek. He was so hot!

She pulled the bedclothes back from his leg and could see what had caused the fever. The bandages were soaked with blood and stained with something thick and yellow. The wound in his leg had broken and the poison was at last escaping.

"Fetch me basins of lukewarm water, quickly!" she snapped at the young man cowering in the shadows. "And some more soft cloths."

"Where shall I – "

"Just bring them, quickly."

Rosanna cut away the bandages and the relief of the pressure seemed to calm the Earl a little.

The next hour flashed past in a blur. Rosanna cleaned the wound again, and constantly laid cooling cloths over his chest and face in an attempt to assuage the fever that wracked his body.

Finally the Earl fell into an uneasy slumber and she sat in a chair by the side of the bed, waiting.

She realised she must have dozed a little because when she came to with a start, the storm had passed and the dawn light was easing through the windows.

She bent over the figure in the bed, her blonde hair escaping from its binding and cascading down over her shoulders in a cloud.

As she placed her hand on the Earl's forehead, his long dark lashes flickered and he was awake, gazing up at her.

"*Angel* – " he muttered, "you've come back to me, *angel*."

"Hush, my Lord," Rosanna urged gently. "You must rest as the poison has drained from your leg and your fever has abated. I think from now on you will soon be on the road to recovery."

"Nurse?" The Earl gazed up at her, unable to grasp that his *angel* had turned into Nurse Robinson.

"Sleep, my Lord," she insisted. "When you wake again, you should feel much better."

She straightened the sheet across his chest but as she moved away, he grasped her hand and held it against his cheek.

Rosanna gasped and stood very still, aware of the

sensation of the Earl's skin under her fingers and the strength of his grip as with a deep sigh, he fell into what she hoped would be a long and healing sleep.

An hour passed and sunlight was streaming in to paint golden puddles on the polished floor when at last the Earl's grip on her hand slackened and Rosanna was able to draw her fingers away.

She sighed as she straightened her back, stiff and sore from the cramped position she had been forced to take so as not to disturb her patient.

The door creaked open behind her and she glanced round to find Mr. Digby.

He beckoned and she followed him out of the bedroom and into a small dressing room next door.

"You must have some sustenance, Nurse Robinson," the elderly man advised firmly. "You have been with his Lordship for many hours, so Simkins informs me."

Rosanna sank down into a chair and closed her eyes. She was so tired! She did not think she had ever felt so exhausted before, even when she had been up all night in London dancing at balls and parties.

But her weariness was laced with a sense of triumph. She knew that she had brought Lord Melton through his crisis and she was overjoyed. He was such an interesting man and one, if her circumstances had been different, she would have been proud to have known better.

She obediently ate the bread and honey that Mr. Digby had laid on a small table and sipped a cup of hot chocolate with relish.

She realised with a start that she was still wearing her nightdress with her old dressing gown over the top. Her feet were bare and dirty and very, very cold.

"Will you sleep, Nurse Robinson?" Mr. Digby asked patiently. "I will watch over his Lordship."

Rosanna nodded. "I will wash and dress and then lie on my bed for a couple of hours. But you must call me instantly if he wakes."

But it was nearly noon before Mr. Digby knocked on her door and told her that the Earl had woken from his sleep.

Rosanna, feeling clean and refreshed, sped down to his bedroom, frowning in trepidation. Had her nursing skills – slight thought they were, helped or hindered? Should she perhaps have called for a doctor to be summoned?

She was delighted by what she found. The Earl was sitting up in bed, his colour was good, his dark eyes were bright and he had obviously been recently shaved.

"Oh, my Lord, I am so pleased to see you looking so much better."

"All thanks to you, Nurse Robinson. I cannot begin to tell you how much improved I feel. This is the first time since my accident that I am free of that dreadful pain in my leg. It aches now, to be sure, but the hellish throbbing has gone."

Rosanna laid a hand on his brow. It was cool and dry under her palm.

"And your fever has broken completely," she smiled.

"I do not recall much about last night," the Earl said, his tone puzzled. "I thought there was someone here – someone I wanted to see. I call her '*my angel*' because she always seems to be around when I need her." Rosanna turned away and busied herself with tidying the room.

"Perhaps you have a real guardian angel," she said lightly, making sure her cap was pulled down firmly over her coiled blonde hair.

The Earl gazed at her sharply. "Perhaps I do," he said quietly and lay watching her slender shape flit around his room, bringing order out of chaos.

"I have never believed in any higher powers," he added slowly. "When my father was alive, I tended to spend all my time finding new ways of losing a goodly part of his fortune. Pain and illness played no part in my selfish world."

Rosanna looked at him, her expression grave.

"I have never been ill myself, but I cared for my mother and – " she paused, remembering suddenly that as a nurse she would have vast knowledge of sickness, " – obviously I have seen other people coping with pain."

"I have lain here this morning vowing to change my ways," the Earl admitted. "I feel I have been given a second chance to make something more of my life."

"I am sure you will succeed, my Lord," Rosanna urged warmly.

She admired him so much for facing up to his past weaknesses. So many people were never aware of the wrong roads they had travelled during their lives and if they were, made no effort to change the path they trod.

"I think I shall try a small adventure today, nurse," the Earl said at last, throwing off his melancholy mood. "I am going to walk around this room and look out of the window. There! Does that sound exciting to you?"

Rosanna smiled, her eyes sparkling.

"It sounds like a very good adventure, my Lord," she agreed. "But I fear you may not walk unaided just yet. Perhaps Simkins – "

Lord Melton groaned and Rosanna gazed at him in alarm.

"Is your leg – ?"

"My leg is still the same, nurse. It is my mind that you need to worry about! The less I see of young Simkins the better. My old valet married a very fine inn-keeper's daughter he met when we were travelling in Italy last year and stayed there as part of her family.

"Simkins was recommended to me by my good friend, Lady Verity Blackwood, but if I am honest, he has not proved very useful during my illness. I feel sure that if I have to lean on him for support, we will both end up on the floor!"

Rosanna tried not to smile at the picture the Earl conjured up. She had to remember that she was supposed to be a servant and as such would not stand exchanging banter and pleasantries with her employer or gossip with him about another member of his staff.

But it was so difficult to remember. Every time she spoke to the Earl, she liked him more and more. She admired his courage and his determination to recover and start his life afresh.

She knew that a lot of men with his money and power would have been happy to have become almost semi-invalids, knowing that everything would be done for them for the rest of their lives.

But what was the point of liking the Earl so much? His very words had just convinced her that his affections lay with Lady Verity Blackwood.

She had picked his last servant and it was obvious that she must be the angel he called for when he was ill.

"So, I plan to have my breakfast – or rather lunch as I fear it is almost midday," the Earl was continuing – "then I will dress and call on you to help me exercise."

"That seems an excellent idea, my Lord."

"And what will you do in the meantime, Nurse Robinson? What do nurses do when their patients are sleeping or eating? Do you study learned tomes about medical matters, perhaps? Or practice rolling bandages or making dressings?"

Rosanna looked up from where she was packing away the contents of her nurse's bag which had become scattered during the course of the night.

Lord Melton was laughing at her! "Oh, we have to find a little cupboard to sit in until we are needed," she replied dryly. "But what I shall do, with your permission, is go for a walk around the castle and take in some much needed fresh air.

"I imagine the storm has cleared away all the heaviness of the past few days and I long to explore. I am so very fond of the countryside."

The Earl nodded. "I remember that you said you prefer it to town living. How I wish I could come with you!"

His handsome face looked grave.

"I would give half my fortune to be able to show you round the castle, point out all my favourite places, then run down to the stable yard and ride Demon up to the Donnington Hall Racecourse."

Rosanna's busy hands stilled as she folded and refolded a heavy linen shirt that had been left lying on the floor.

"Donnington Hall? Is that the big house I passed on my way to the castle?" she remarked casually. "A few miles away from here."

"Yes, that's right. A lovely house. The late owner, Sir Leonard Donnington, was a good friend of my father.

"I knew him slightly myself, but not well because I have been away travelling in Europe for many years. But Sir Leonard built a marvellous Racecourse up at Donnington and I had permission for my own horses to exercise there whenever I so wished."

"Do you know the present owner?" Rosanna asked mischievously.

The Earl shook his head. "No, I have not yet had that pleasure. The estate has passed to some little niece, a mere child. I expect her friends and advisers will sell it for her.

"I believe she lives in London and is probably one of those flighty young girls who wants for nothing in life but dresses and dances and – and new bonnets!"

"New bonnets are very important, my Lord," Rosanna admitted gravely, trying to stop herself from giggling.

The Earl waved his hand dismissively. "Lot of trivial nonsense!" he asserted. "But I am convinced she won't be interested in horses and Racecourses!"

Rosanna threw open the window to let in more fresh air.

"I am sure you are right, my Lord," she agreed, crossing her fingers as she spoke, remembering how Martha, her old Scottish nanny, had told her that if you did this when telling a lie, it didn't count as one!

"Well, if you will excuse me, my Lord. I will ring for Simkins to come and help you dress and while you are thus occupied, I will go outside to breathe the good fresh country air."

The Earl watched her go. It was good to feel a little better and he knew that he had Nurse Robinson to thank.

But he had to admit she puzzled him greatly. Her voice, her vocabulary, even the graceful way she moved – everything about her spoke of an education and upbringing that a nurse, no matter how dedicated, would not have achieved.

He compared her good sense and bravery in dealing with his injury to that of Verity who had run away to London, unable to cope with his declining health.

'Although perhaps that is an unfair comparison,' he murmured to himself. 'After all, Verity is a lady with refined sensibilities and should not be expected to do and see such things.'

But that thought left the Earl even more bewildered, because Nurse Robinson seemed to him to have as much if not more sensitivity than her social betters.

'Perhaps she is from a good family who have fallen on hard times,' he pondered. He did realise that if a father or brother lost all his money in business or gambling, the wives and daughters were forced into working to keep body and soul together.

'I must try and discover her secret,' he thought as Simkins arrived with clean clothes and he began the long and weary task of dressing.

'There may be some way in which I can help her in the future – for there is no doubt that I owe her my life. Perhaps I can recommend her to friends who are in need of a nurse. A long-term position in a stately home would surely be of benefit to her.'

And he pushed to the back of his mind the random thought that if only she had been a lady of his own social standing, his admiration for Nurse Robinson could have developed into something far stronger.

Outside in the warm sunshine, Rosanna was enjoying the glorious day. The storm had washed away dust and grime from bushes and trees and every leaf and every flower petal seemed to quiver with bright life in the gentle breeze.

She walked across the moat and down through fields thick with buttercups and daisies to where the racehorses were grazing in a series of large white fenced paddocks.

"Oh, how kind of someone," she gasped, because there was her little fat pony, Smudger, grazing happily alongside the beautiful bloodstock that she knew were worth hundreds of guineas each.

At the sound of her voice, the pony raised his grey head and after solemnly staring at her as he chewed a mouthful of grass, he ambled over and pushed his velvety nose against her hands, searching for any little titbit she might have had for him.

"Sorry, little pony. I have nothing to give you, I'm afraid. I never dreamed you would be out here in such grand company."

Rosanna smoothed his mane and gazed out over the fields where the long grasses shimmered in the sunlight.

How lovely it would be to ride today, to feel the breeze cooling her face. Suddenly a wicked idea flashed into her head. There was no one around, no one to see.

She opened the gate, led Smudger through and made sure the latch was tightly down. The race horses watched in interest as she hitched up her long grey skirt and vaulted up onto the pony's broad back.

Rosanna laughed out loud. She was showing an enormous amount of white cotton stocking – right up to above her knees – but she had been taught to ride without a saddle by Clive, her dear brother, when they were children and the pony held no fears for her.

'It is a very good thing that Lord Melton cannot see his nurse at this very moment. I fear he would find my behaviour extremely strange and unladylike!'

She tangled her hands in the rough grey mane and turned the pony's head out towards the open countryside.

'We'll just walk over to that big grove of trees,' she whispered softly. 'There's no one to see us and in half an hour I can have you safely back in the paddock with no harm done.'

Smudger certainly seemed to appreciate being on the move. He walked swiftly forward when she kicked him softly with her heels, eager to stretch his legs.

Rosanna sighed with pleasure. After her traumatic and busy night, the worry over Lord Melton and having to play-act all the time in front of him and the staff, it was sheer Heaven to be out here on her own, able to enjoy the beautiful scenery with not a care in the world for a few minutes.

They reached the trees with no problems and Rosanna was pleased as the cool green shade shut out the glare from the sun. Smudger drifted to a halt and lowered his shaggy head to crop the grass.

'What an odd and yet enthralling few days I have had since leaving London,' she thought. 'How far away now that life of balls and gossip, visits and shopping seems. I truly believe that if I could just return to Donnington Hall and rid myself of Sir Walter, I would never need to visit London again.'

Her blue eyes became troubled as all her problems came to the forefront of her mind once more.

Escaping to Melton Castle had seemed like such a good idea, but now she realised that her close proximity to Lord Melton had opened up a new avenue of worry.

She admitted that flight had been the only thing in her mind when she fled from her home. But at some point she would have to confess who she was to the Earl. There was no way she could let him continue to believe she was a nurse.

Eventually, whatever happened, they would meet socially and she knew that she would be extremely disturbed and unhappy if she ever saw condemnation and even disgust in his dark eyes.

"But why should it matter to me what he thinks?" she said out loud. "Even if I continue to live at Donnington Hall, there is no need for us to meet socially. Indeed, I imagine the Earl will marry his angel, Lady Verity Blackwood, and spend a great deal of his time in London with her."

Just as her thoughts were growing darker and darker, Smudger threw up his head and snorted. He had heard, seconds before Rosanna could, hoof beats on the path through the wood – someone was coming and at a gallop.

Rosanna gulped and turned the pony, intent on getting out of the way. But even as she kicked Smudger into action, a horse thundered round the bend and was reined to a skidding halt, its rider yelling and cursing as he hauled on the reins.

And to Rosanna's horror, she recognised the horse and rider immediately. It was Sir Walter Fenwick!

There was no doubting the man's skill as an equestrian. He kept his seat, spun the horse round and then, with a sinking heart, as she kicked her pony into a trot, she heard him call out,

"Lady Rosanna? Is that you? By God it is. Lady Rosanna! Come back! Come back at once."

Rosanna refused to look round. All he could have seen was her back view, but she had thrown off her nurse's cap when she left the castle and her long blonde hair was cascading over her shoulders.

She urged the pony into a canter but knew there was no way she could outrun Sir Walter's horse. Oh, this was dreadful! All her schemes and plans would be for nothing if he was certain it was her.

Bending low over Smudger's mane, Rosanna urged him off the path and he obediently jumped a small log and pushed his way into the thick undergrowth.

With dainty steps, he made his way through the bushes, under tree branches that were so near the ground that Rosanna had to lie almost flat to pass under them, feeling leaves and twigs catch in her hair as she did so.

But she knew that Sir Walter could never force his big hunter to follow her. She could hear him shouting and calling, but at last they broke out of the woods and she shook Smudger into a wild gallop down the hill and across the fields, back towards the castle.

Leaning low over his ears, Rosanna urged the little pony to go faster, faster! They sped past the paddocks, but she knew there would be no time to put the pony back with the other horses.

She could hear hooves behind her, thundering on the dry track. Sir Walter was in hot pursuit!

The pony clattered over the wooden ramp across the moat, towards the stables. Rosanna leapt off his back, gazing round wildly. She could hear the man she hated so much, still calling her name. In seconds he would be across the moat and in the stable yard.

There was no time to run into the castle. She was trapped!

"My Lady! My Lady! Over here. Quickly!"

Rosanna spun round, unable to believe her eyes. There in the doorway of a cottage, red curls gleaming, was Edie, her maid.

She was beckoning urgently.

Then John Barker appeared at a run, pulled Smudger by his mane and led him away into the stable block.

Her head whirling, Rosanna ran for the cottage and sanctuary.

The door had just closed behind her when a scarlet-faced Sir Walter, using his whip viciously on his chestnut hunter, came galloping into the stable yard and skidded to a halt.

He leapt off his mount, cursing, his gooseberry-coloured eyes bulging with anger. A great vein pulsed in his forehead and there was spittle on his lips.

"Lady Rosanna! I know it was you riding the grey pony. Come out, madam! This is your fiancé speaking. I demand that you come out of hiding and face me at once!"

CHAPTER SEVEN

Inside the little cottage, Rosanna collapsed onto a chair as Edie slammed the door shut and locked it. Her copper-headed maid stood defiantly in front of her Mistress, her fists clenched, and even in her anguish, Rosanna could smile at the sight of the slim slip of a girl preparing to defend her against all comers.

Outside, they could hear Sir Walter shouting, the stamping of hooves and then John Barker's firm quiet voice.

"I am sorry, Sir Walter, but there's no Lady Rosanna here."

"Nonsense! I saw her ride in here with my own eyes. She was on a grey pony. Let me pass! I am Sir Walter Fenwick and I wish to search these stables at once."

Rosanna flinched. If he found the pony, he would know he was right. How long would it take him to make the head groom tell him where she was hiding?

"Don't you fret none, my Lady," Edie whispered. "John won't tell him nothing. Just you wait and see."

"But the pony – "

"One of the lads will have trotted him down to the far paddock. He'll be fine. We just have to sit and wait."

Minutes passed, then Rosanna heard Sir Walter cursing violently as he strode out of the stable block.

"Damn your hide, man. I will see you pay for thwarting me in this fashion. You're hiding my fiancée somewhere, I know you are!"

"Sir Walter – "

"What's in here? Did she run inside this hovel when she got back to the castle?"

To Rosanna's horror, the door shook as Sir Walter rattled the handle violently, but the lock held.

"Why is this door locked? What are you hiding?"

"Why nothing, Sir Walter. My little girl is alone inside and I don't want her running off. She is suffering from a bad attack of fever, but don't let that stop you looking if you want to, sir. Here, let me unlock it – "

"Fever? No, no, that won't be necessary – "

His voice dwindled away and Rosanna breathed more easily as she heard the sound of his horse's hooves on the cobbles.

"Listen, whatever you say, I know Lady Rosanna is here at Melton Castle," he said. "I will be back. And when I do, you will be sorry you have obstructed me in this fashion."

And at last came the sound of a horse moving away, out of the stable yard.

"He's gone, my Lady," Edie said, pulling back the corner of the yellow flowered curtain at the little window and peering out.

"Oh, thank God. I have never seen anyone so angry. He seemed – Edie – he seemed quite mad, chasing me across country. If he had caught me – I cannot bear to think of it!"

She shuddered and dropped her head in her hands.

"Don't take on so, my Lady. Here, a nice cup of tea is what you need."

Rosanna lifted her head and smiled, reluctantly. Edie's

answer to every problem in life from a lost button to a dreadful tragedy was always, 'a nice cup of tea.'

"Thank you, Edie. That would be lovely. I am so delighted to see you, but surprised. Did you not go to Donnington Hall?"

Edie nodded and told Rosanna her story – how Sir Walter had dismissed her when she said she had no idea where Rosanna was, how Bates had slipped her a note suggesting she head for Melton Castle and her adventure with John Barker's little daughter.

"But you cannot be staying here with them, surely?" Rosanna asked, distressed for the younger girl's reputation.

Edie smiled and shook her head.

"Oh, no, my Lady. I have a room just off the stable block. I was hiding there until I could manage to speak to you."

Rosanna sipped her tea. It was indeed hot and sweet and reviving.

"So John Barker knows I am living in the castle, pretending to be a nurse," she enquired anxiously.

Edie nodded, her red curls shaking vigorously. "Oh, don't worry, my Lady. John won't say a word. He'll have me to answer for if he does!"

Rosanna sighed and stood up.

"He is a good man, Edie. And you are a brave girl to have tracked me down here. But soon I shall have to go back to Donnington Hall and face my problems. Sir Walter isn't going to leave and return to London as I thought he would."

Edie gave a disdainful sniff.

"If you ask me, my Lady, he can see the pot of gold at the end of the rainbow. You must be very careful. He's got a bad reputation, that one, and he loves his horses and gambling."

Rosanna smoothed her long grey skirt, trying to bring some order back to her nurse's uniform that had been badly creased from her whirlwind ride.

"He frightens me, Edie," she said gravely, "I do believe he is insane – indeed he seems that way, especially when he cannot get his own way. But I swear on everything I hold dear that I will not be bullied into marrying him. No woman should be forced into an alliance against her will."

Edie was busy washing up the used cup and saucer, her back to her Mistress.

"And will you be telling Lord Melton who you are, my Lady?"

Rosanna hesitated. She knew that she must confess to the Earl, and soon, but it was going to be such a difficult conversation. And she worried about his health. Was he strong enough yet to be confronted with such news?

Would he perhaps view her as a charlatan, someone not to be trusted, order her out of his castle, and insist that she return to her own home? The very thought made her tremble with unhappiness.

But why should she react in this way? She had only known the Earl for a short while and his affections were so obviously engaged elsewhere – with the woman he called 'his angel.'

Rosanna gave herself a mental shake.

"Yes, indeed that is something I have to do soon, Edie. But for now, I need to return to my room and check on my patient. I have been gone too long for a casual walk in the fresh air."

Edie glanced swiftly at her Mistress's flushed cheeks and for once held her tongue. 'Oh, ho,' she thought with glee, 'that's how the land lies, eh? Well, I'm not a bit surprised, but I only hope he feels the same way about her.'

A quick check into the stable yard convinced Rosanna that Sir Walter had indeed left the castle.

With swift orders to Edie to remain where she was until further notice, she hurried into the castle and fled up the stone stairways and along the vast corridors to her bedroom.

She splashed her face with cold water from the blue and white basin and did her best to tie up her long blonde hair so it sat neatly under the nurse's cap.

But her reflection in the small dressing table mirror showed someone who looked flushed and excited.

Swiftly Rosanna changed her filthy apron for a clean one, relying on it covering the worst of the stains and snags her dress had gathered from the wild ride through the woods.

There was no time to change her stockings and shoes and she would just have to hope that the Earl would be too preoccupied with his health to notice.

Dusk was falling by the time she made her way downstairs to the Earl's bedroom. She tapped gently on the door, but there was no reply.

Opening it, she was surprised and worried to find the big room empty.

"Oh, Nurse Robinson, there you are! Why have you been away from your post for so long? His Lordship has been asking for you for the past hour."

The butler, Mr. Digby was standing there, looking at her with a disapproving expression.

"I am so sorry, I lost track of the time," she explained hastily. "But where is Lord Melton? He has surely not been able to walk far. He will do his leg some permanent damage if he does."

Mr Digby's expression softened at the note of real concern in the young woman's voice. He found it refreshing. All the other nurses who had come to the castle, had been good women, but to them the Earl had been just another patient and they had not shown a great deal of compassion.

"His Lordship is in the small blue drawing room, nurse. In the end turret of the castle."

"Thank you, Mr. Digby," Rosanna said and hurried along the stone passageway. Her knock at the door was greeted by a command to enter.

She found the Earl seated on the window seat in front of a curved window that looked out over the grounds and far away into the distance.

He was dressed in a white shirt and grey trousers. He had been shaved and his dark hair was brushed back, except for one unruly lock that fell across his forehead. He looked far better than he had earlier that morning.

"Ah, Nurse Robinson. You have returned from your walk refreshed, I hope?"

"I must apologise for being back so late, my Lord," Rosanna said, hurrying across to him. "I am afraid I went further than I had planned."

The Earl smiled up at her and she was delighted to see that colour had returned to his cheeks and his dark eyes were bright.

"No matter. You are here now. I imagine you are surprised to find me up and about."

"Indeed, my Lord, it is a delight to behold, but I do hope you are not overtaxing your strength. Your fever was very bad."

The Earl waved away her concerns. "Apart from a faint ache in my leg where the wound is healing, I feel incredibly better. And it is all due to your skill, nurse."

He looked at her sharply.

"Where did you train? I am sure our local hospital would be glad to acquire nurses of your ability. And I have various friends who are also in need of a live-in nurse. I would be pleased to recommend you. Just say the word."

Rosanna bit her lip and took a step backwards. This was dreadful. How could she go on lying to him? But what could she say? Was this the right time to tell the truth?

She took a deep breath and stared down into those warm, honest eyes. He was too fine a man to cheat in this fashion. Whatever he thought of her, he must know the truth at once.

"My Lord, I must tell you – "

"Do you like this room, nurse?" the Earl interrupted her and she stopped in mid-sentence, startled.

"Yes, indeed, my Lord. It is very fine."

He was looking around at the odd, circular room. Pale blue silk curtains softened the old grey stones and there were soft Persian rugs on the floor.

The Earl nodded now to the far corner. "This was my mother's drawing room. That is her piano."

Rosanna walked across and touched the keys with gentle fingers.

"It is a lovely instrument. Did she die many years ago, my Lord?"

He sighed and replied quietly,

"I was just ten. I have good memories of her. I remember my governess bringing me here in the afternoon and Digby – a much younger Digby, of course! – serving tea for me and my parents. My mother would play and sing and we were happy. After her death, I was sent to Eton."

Rosanna glanced back at him, but he was outlined against the window and in the shadow she could not see the expression on his face.

Her heart ached for him. She had lost her mother recently and the scars from the grief were still raw. But at least she had been an adult when the loss occurred. Lord Melton had been but a child and left to the devices of a busy father and the brisk impersonal life of a boarding-school, she could imagine his loss had seemed the greater.

"Do you play the piano, by any chance, nurse?"

Rosanna hesitated. Of course Lady Rosanna Donnington had been given music lessons since she was five, but would a Nurse Robinson have had the same advantages?

Then as he stood up and walked towards her, she could see his face clearly. He looked so sad, so wistful, that she threw caution to the winds and sat down at the beautiful piano.

"I haven't played for some time, my Lord," she said. "But this is a little tune that my mother liked very much."

The soft notes of a little French lullaby fell into the room like drops of cool water falling into a fountain on a hot day.

The Earl crossed the room and leant on the piano, staring down at the hideous white cap covering a knot of blonde hair and her hands with those long sensitive fingers gently caressing the keys.

'Well,' he thought as he enjoyed the delicate music, 'I do not know who you are, Nurse Robinson, but you are *not* a nurse. You are a lady born and bred. Those hands have never done hard work day after day. I wonder why you will not confide in me?'

"That was excellent," he said as the piece came to an end. "Charming. You play very well, nurse."

Rosanna stood and began to tidy the music that lay on top of the piano.

"No, my Lord, I think I need a great deal more practice to be considered a good player. But I know enough to entertain myself – when I have access to a piano, that is!"

"Of course."

He smiled, watching her long, slim hands bringing order to the sheet music. Small tendrils of hair were escaping from under her cap and he could see how fine and blonde they were.

He felt a desperate desire to see what her hair would be like if it was unpinned from its severe style and set free from that dreadful cap.

"I find music very soothing, especially when I am suffering from some mental affliction. It helps me to concentrate on finding a way out of my difficulties."

The Earl's dark brown eyes sharpened.

"Are you suggesting I should have more music in my life, nurse?"

Rosanna flushed but turned to face him. She would not flinch.

"I think music and prayer are a great help, my Lord. I feel that most people today are rather inclined to say, 'oh, well, it has happened and we can do nothing about it.' I am sure that is wrong."

"I am sure it is wrong, too," the Earl agreed and she was aware of just how close they were standing. She could see where a button was hanging by a thread from his shirt and had to stop herself from reaching out to pull it free.

"You seem to think in a very different way from most women, Nurse Robinson. You are extremely sensible for one so young. Surely you should be doing something better with your life than looking after ill people such as myself?"

Rosanna turned away. She did not want him to see the guilt she sensed must be written on her face.

"I feel that nursing is a very worthwhile occupation, my Lord. Perhaps if more girls of good education followed that calling, then more good would be done for the sick and injured."

Lord Melton frowned. "You will be saying you want women to become doctors, too, and cut up bodies and perform dreadful operations!"

Rosanna spun back, her chin up, her blue eyes flashing.

"Any woman who would have the courage to walk such a path would have my utmost admiration."

There was silence for a second. Rosanna gasped. She had forgotten who she was supposed to be. No mere employee would have dreamed of speaking to the Earl in such tones, no matter how provoked.

"Forgive me, my Lord. I spoke without thinking. All I meant was that we should all use the brains we have been given by God and not neglect them in pursuit of ephemeral ideas that might leave us disillusioned and unhappy."

The Earl listened to her, staring down at the beautiful face before him.

"Who are you really, Nurse Robinson?" he asked vehemently and just then there was a knock at the door and Digby entered.

"There's a gentleman downstairs to see you, my Lord. His name is Sir Walter Fenwick and he says that although you have never been introduced, it is very important he should see you. He knows you have been ill, but still insists on a minute or two of your time. He would not be sent away, my Lord."

Rosanna swayed and gulped in horror.

"Oh, no!" she cried. "He is looking for me, but I cannot see him. Please help me!"

The Earl and Digby both stared at her, astonished by her outburst.

"Do you know this man?" Lord Melton asked.

"I know him and the reason he is here. He wants to

take me away and it will be difficult for me to refuse him, he scares me so much," she replied in a flurry.

"I can send him away, but he may come back another time, or he may watch the castle if he is so keen on seeing you. What hold does he have over you, nurse?"

"Please, please, just send him away, my Lord, and I will explain everything."

She spoke in such a pleading voice that the Earl looked at her in surprise.

"I will see him. Digby, show him up. Nurse Robinson – that Chinese screen by the far wall is large enough to hide a small person such as yourself. Sit on the chair behind it and you can listen and not be seen. Do not fret, I will not let him near you."

Her face as white as her cap, Rosanna took up her position.

The Earl turned to his butler. "Now show Sir Walter Fenwick upstairs, but remember, do not mention that I have a nurse living in the castle. If he inquires from you, say my leg is rebandaged every day by staff from the hospital."

His footsteps died away and when the room was empty, Rosanna heard the Earl walk across to the screen and say quietly,

"You have no need to be frightened. I will not let this man harm you in any way. Trust me."

"Oh, I do," Rosanna whispered desperately, clasping her hands in her lap in anguish.

"If it is the Devil himself, he will not take you against your will," the Earl muttered as he returned to his seat. "Not while I have a breath left in my body."

Minutes later Rosanna heard the door open and Digby announce in a cold, disdainful tone,

"Sir Walter Fenwick to see you, my Lord."

Rosanna shuddered as the harsh voice she hated so much rang out.

"Forgive me for intruding in this way, but I need your assistance, sir, and I am sure you are able to help me."

Lord Melton had retired to a large chair and through the narrow gap that existed between the two parts of the screen, Rosanna could see that he was lying back on the heavily embroidered blue cushions with his foot propped up on a stool.

"To help you, sir? I am afraid at the moment I am too ill after a fall from my horse to help anyone. I am at present confined to this floor of the castle as I cannot manage the stairs."

As Rosanna watched, Sir Walter strode forward and stood next to the Earl. The very sight of his squat form, the broad shoulders straining at the seams of his tawny jacket and the strands of his greasy hair clinging to his thick freckled neck, made her feel sick and faint.

"I have it on good authority that a certain nurse, who I am very anxious to speak with, has come here to assist you."

The Earl did not speak. He just looked faintly bored.

After a moment, Sir Walter resumed, "I have also learnt that the nurse arrived riding a small grey pony. I have, in fact, seen a similar pony today in your paddock. It is the only pony you have amongst your horses. It must have come from her house to the castle, which is why I am here."

There was a long silence and then the Earl spoke at last, in rather lofty, bored tones, the voice of a young aristocrat who could not be bothered to pay proper interest to his visitor, quite unlike his usual concise way of speaking.

"I think you must be referring to a woman who came to me for a day or so after I dismissed those who were sent from the local hospital. They seemed inefficient to me and I was recommended to a nurse who happened to be staying nearby with friends, breaking her journey south to the coast."

Rosanna could see through her spy hole that the back of Sir Walter's neck had gone bright red.

When he replied, his voice was curt and angry.

"The nurse who is attending you at the moment is, I understand, quite young and pretty and is not a real nurse, just pretending to be one."

Again there was silence, before the Earl said,

"I am afraid, Sir Walter, that you have been misinformed. The nurse I engaged for a few days has now left. She asked me to stable her pony for her as she was going to France. Naturally she could not take it with her."

"Do you expect me to believe that this particular young woman is no longer here at the castle?"

"Damn it, man, you can believe what you choose. She was here for two nights and then she continued on her journey to France."

Sir Walter drew in his breath. "Are you telling me the truth? I find it hard to believe."

Rosanna bit back a gasp. This was tantamount to calling Lord Melton a liar! Duels had been fought over such remarks and there was no way the Earl was fit enough to take on Sir Walter, even if he was a fine shot, which she was sure he would be.

She half rose from her chair. This was dreadful. She could not allow his health to be compromised in such a fashion. She cared too much for him. She would have to confront Sir Walter and cope with the consequences.

But the Earl was obviously not about to be pushed into any rash action by the older man.

"Sir Walter, I will ignore that last remark and pretend you did not say it. You are obviously upset and we all say things in moments of stress that we regret at a later date.

"But let me make it quite clear, you are wasting both your time and mine, sir. There is no nurse here at the castle. I give you my word as a gentleman and if that is not enough for you, I shall be forced to take the matter further."

Sir Walter's face became contorted with fury and his voice was almost hoarse with anger.

"I suppose you know that although she was pretending to be a nurse, she is really Lady Rosanna Donnington, heiress to Sir Leonard Donnington, a great friend of your late father. She has disappeared from Donnington Hall in the most extraordinary and unusual circumstances."

Lord Melton stood up and limped to the window, staring out across the castle grounds.

"You must forgive me if I enquire why you are so anxious to find this lady?"

"I am not only anxious, I am determined to do so," Sir Walter snapped in tones that sounded worse because they were so cold. "Lady Rosanna belongs to me. Do you hear? We are to be married next week. The church is booked, the date set. She will be my wife before the month ends!"

CHAPTER EIGHT

Sitting behind the ornamental screen, Rosanna bit back a scream. She dug her fingers into her palms so hard that the nails almost broke her skin.

How dare Sir Walter speak like that? Arrange their marriage without her consent. It was ridiculous. No one could be forced to marry against their will, surely?

But at the back of her mind, she felt a flicker of fear and doubt. He was so ruthless, so strong. What if he drugged her with laudanum and she woke to find herself Lady Fenwick? She had read stories of girls being spirited off to Arabian countries as part of what she knew was called 'the white slave trade'.

How easy it would be for Sir Walter to arrange something similar to happen to her once she left the protection of Melton Castle and returned home to Donnington Hall.

Then, like water falling onto parched ground, Rosanna heard the Earl speaking. And the languid, aristocratic drawl had vanished. His voice was terse and crisp, ringing with sincerity.

"I am afraid that I have nothing further to say on this matter, Sir Walter. You speak of this lady 'belonging' to you, as if she is no more than a piece of porcelain or a saddle and bridle. I am afraid I can have no part in this and – as you can see – I have rung for my butler to show you out."

Through the gap between the two parts of the screen, Rosanna watched as Mr. Digby politely, but disdainfully, held open the door.

Sir Walter pushed his way past him with a snarl, but turned on his heel to confront Lord Melton once more.

"You will be sorry for this, Melton," he hissed, his florid face purple with rage, little flecks of spittle settling on his chin.

"I don't know what game you are playing, but I reckon you've got your eye on Lady Rosanna Donnington and the Donnington Racecourse. That's it, isn't it? Be a nice little addition to your estate, wouldn't it? The land and the house and a pretty, biddable girl to take to your bed.

"And once you had full access to the Racecourse, your horses would be far superior to all others. Well, you won't win! I will see to that. Just watch your back!"

And then he was gone and Rosanna could have sworn that the whole room seemed lighter and fresher with his departure.

Taking a deep breath, because now was the moment of accountability, she stepped out from behind the screen.

The Earl turned and gazed down at her, his expression unreadable.

Rosanna lifted her chin and gazed at the man who, so recently, had been her patient. She was not scared. She knew him too well. He was kind and honest and even if he was angry with her, she knew he would treat her with courtesy.

He bowed, formally.

"Lady Rosanna Donnington."

She dropped him a brief curtsy.

"Lord Melton."

His lips twitched and he held out his hand.

"This is indeed a strange meeting, madam. You are strangely similar to the nurse who has looked after me so well during my recent illness. Indeed, you could almost be sisters!"

Rosanna looked up into his dark eyes and with a surge of relief saw they were not angry at all, but twinkling with laughter.

"Perhaps she comes from another branch of my family, my Lord!"

"Indeed, perhaps she does!" Then the merriment died from his face and he led her to the window seat.

Rosanna sank down on the blue velvet cushions and said,

"I must apologise most sincerely, Lord Melton, for deceiving you in such a fashion. Believe me, I would not have entered into this disguise if I'd had any other choice. I only hope that my lack of nursing skills has not harmed you in any way."

She bit her lip.

"I appreciate that my behaviour has been – well – not what you would expect from a lady of my standing. I can only guess at what my dear departed Mama would have said had been alive to see me. But, my Lord, my circumstances have been so dire – I needed to escape from – well you heard that dreadful man's words, you can see what I was trying to escape."

Lord Melton sat beside her, wincing a little as the wound on his leg still had the power to hurt him.

"Madam, if it would not cause you too much pain, I would be grateful if you could enlighten me as to what has transpired. I take it, of course, that you *are* Lady Rosanna, the new owner of Donnington Hall."

Rosanna nodded and swiftly told her story – of her vast inheritance from her great-uncle, the various marriage proposals that had so swiftly come her way from fortune hunters, Sir Walter's insistence that she become his wife, her flight to the country and Sir Walter's dogged pursuit.

Rosanna shuddered. "He is hateful, appalling. He is so determined to marry me, but at the root of his obsession is my money and the Racecourse and horses at Donnington Hall. He talks of nothing else."

She felt herself blushing. "Indeed, I know that is what drives him on. It is not my person. I am not so vain as to believe I have that sort of power to attract a man."

Lord Melton ran his fingers through his dark, unruly hair, looking grave. He had sensed a wild, almost insane quality to Sir Walter's behaviour that was unsettling even to him. He could only imagine how terrifying it would seem to a young lady.

The fact that this particular young lady seated next to him had actually succeeded in foiling her pursuer twice was not lost on him.

"You say your maid is living in my stables?" he said now, turning to the second incredible part of her story.

"Edie Robinson, yes. It was her name I took for mine! In the heat of the moment I could think of no other. Sir Walter threw her out of Donnington Hall when she arrived from London and she made her way here."

She smiled warmly. "Indeed, I think your head groom has taken a fancy to her and she to him! There is, apparently, a little room at the end of the stables where records are kept. She is sleeping there, but seems to spend most of her time in John Barker's cottage taking care of his little daughter!"

Lord Melton frowned. He was just beginning to realise how much had been going on at the castle without his knowledge while he had been so ill.

"Oh, please don't be angry with John!" Rosanna begged, correctly guessing what the expression on his face meant. "He only wanted to help, and believe me, Edie can be very persuasive."

Lord Melton gazed down into her cornflower blue eyes and reluctantly smiled. It was very hard to say no to this young woman, sitting there so prim and proper in her over large nurse's uniform.

He reached over and tweaked her severe white cap with one long finger.

"Do you need to keep that monstrosity on your head now that your identity has been revealed?"

Rosanna blushed and reaching up her hand, pulled off the nurse's head-dress. As it came away, it caught at the pins holding up her hair and her golden locks tumbled down around her shoulders like a cloud of blonde spun sugar.

Lord Melton gasped and stared at her, his dark eyes wide with astonishment.

"Why, you're my *angel*!" he cried. "The vision who looked after me at the inn on my way home from Bath when I was feeling so ill!"

Rosanna nodded.

"I was travelling to Donnington Hall for the very first time, my Lord. One of the horses lost a shoe, so we stopped at the inn while he was shod. I was so worried to see a gentleman so cast down by affliction, lying alone and unattended."

Lord Melton bowed his head. "I am in your debt, Lady Rosanna. Indeed, I have something of yours I must return."

Rosanna looked at him in puzzlement as he reached into his breeches pocket and pulled out a small, crumpled white handkerchief edged with fine lace.

"This is yours, I believe," he said, his eyes sparkling. "You used it to mop my brow and I have kept it by me ever since."

Rosanna stood up and dropped him a small curtsy. "Thank you, sir," she whispered as she held out her hand to take it.

Lord Melton stared down into eyes that were deep and honest. He was shocked by the flood of emotion he experienced as their fingers touched.

Feelings were racing through him that he had never experienced. But it was far too soon to declare himself to this young woman. And – he realised with a shock – they were alone, unchaperoned and she was no longer his nurse.

Suddenly there was a commotion in the passageway outside. A strident female voice could be heard.

"Get out of my way, Digby. Of course Lord Melton is at home to me. What rubbish!"

"Verity Blackwood!" the Earl snapped. "She must not find us alone, Lady Rosanna. Your reputation will suffer if she does."

With a gasp of horror, Rosanna spun away, cramming her hair into the nurse's cap which she pulled down over her ears as far as she could.

She picked up a cushion that had fallen on the floor and tried to look busy tidying the room.

Lord Melton just had time to lie back in his chair when the door flew open and Lady Verity stalked in. Wearing an elegant riding costume in dark green, with lace at the neck, she was tall and stately, every inch the aristocratic lady.

Rosanna felt very small and grubby in her dark grey uniform. But she only hoped that the very plainness of her garb meant she would fade successfully into the background.

"William, how good it is to see you again and looking so much better," Verity said, dropping an elegant bob and extending her gloved hand to the Earl.

He touched her hand briefly.

"Lady Verity. A pleasure, madam. What brings you back to Melton Castle. Is George with you?"

Lady Verity tossed her head and sat down next to him, saying,

"I am staying with Sir James and Lady Carling, my aunt and uncle. They live just ten miles away, as you know. My brother refused to leave London. His affairs – which seem to involve a gambling club – require his constant attendance."

"Surely you are not alone, madam? It is very late to be travelling on horseback."

Lady Verity smiled. "I thank you for your concern, William. Of course I would never ride out alone. I was accompanied by a groom. Indeed, I did not mean to ride so far from Carling Manor, but the beauty of your estate led me further and further afield until it became too dark to turn back. I knew I could throw myself on your hospitality without fear of refusal."

She leant over and touched his sleeve. "I presume that you will not turn me out into the night, sir? A bed for the evening is all I crave."

Rosanna gulped and dropped the books she was putting into neat piles.

Lady Verity stared round at her, taking in the small, slim figure in dark grey who was standing quietly in a corner, her hands clasped demurely in front of her apron, her eyes cast down to the floor, a picture of a model servant – or so Rosanna hoped. As long as the tendrils of hair she could feel escaping down her neck were not visible to the Society lady!

"Aha, Lord Melton, I am sure you would not wish to converse in front of your nurse. You – woman – leave us."

Rosanna glanced up at the dark haired Earl. His face was impassive but she could see his hands clenching on the arms of the chair.

She knew instinctively that rudeness to servants was something he would never indulge in himself and it was only his politeness to a guest that had stopped him making a terse remark to Lady Verity.

"If you would be so kind, Nurse Robinson," he said and Rosanna dropped a little curtsy and hurried out of the room, her head down, aware of Lady Verity's sharp eyes following her as she left.

She hastened along the stone corridor back to her room, wondering what she should do now.

She could no longer carry on this deception in front of the staff, but how could she just announce who she was? What would Mr. Digby and Peter Simkins think when they knew?

She had not intended to make fools of these people and, of course, she might never need to see them again, but she was anxious not to hurt their feelings.

She had no clothes to wear, except those of the nurse and she could not see any way of bringing her possessions from Donnington Hall without alerting Sir Walter as to her whereabouts. And that was the last thing she wanted.

Rosanna sank down onto the little stool in front of her dressing table and stared at her reflection in the small, smeared mirror. Impatiently, she pulled off the wretched cap and let her hair fall to her shoulders once more.

She thrust her hand into her apron pocket and pulled out the scrap of linen and lace that the Earl had returned to her. She shut her eyes and raised the handkerchief to her lips.

She could not believe that Lord Melton had kept this little token. It was such an impossible thing to have happened that she had difficulty in making her brain accept it. What could it mean?

She picked up her hair brush and slowly began the

hundred strokes that her mother had insisted she performed each evening.

Well, of course his behaviour means nothing, she thought crossly. And it was stupid of her to read more into his action than he intended. He had been pleased that a stranger helped him when he was ill, but now he knew who that stranger was, the token would mean nothing to him.

And especially when Lady Verity had arrived back to claim her rightful place in his affections.

She was tall, stately and elegant, everything Rosanna knew she was not. There was no way that Lady Verity would be intimidated by a man such as Sir Walter.

Rosanna banged the silver hair brush against her scalp and winced. And that, she told herself angrily, was the reason her eyes were beginning to water and tears were brimming over her lashes. It had nothing to do with Lord Melton and his feelings for the other woman who obviously meant a lot to him.

'I must make a plan,' Rosanna decided firmly. 'I ran away to give myself space in which to think, but the time is coming when I shall have to face Sir Walter and make a stand.

'I shall fetch Edie and we will return to Donnington Hall tomorrow, as soon as it is light. I will be courteous to Sir Walter, but firm. I will make it very clear that I shall never agree to be his wife and if he refuses to leave I will – I will – call for the local constabulary!'

With that, Rosanna slapped her hair brush down on the dressing table. The reflection in the mirror had changed from a sad, hesitant, timid looking girl to one whose chin was high, whose blue eyes were sparkling with resolve and determination.

She refused to think of all the problems that might lie ahead. Now she just wanted to go home to Donnington Hall, to leave the castle and the Earl behind. She had no desire to watch him with his lady.

Suddenly the tears in her eyes brimmed over and ran down her cheeks unheeded as she realised with horror that she would rather face the dreadful Sir Walter than watch Lord Melton parade around this fine place with Lady Verity on his arm!

*

Very early the next morning, Lady Verity hurried down the great staircase, her head held high and her eyes blazing with anger.

How dare he! How dare Lord Melton throw away their relationship with just a few bleak words.

She pushed past a footman who jumped to open the main doors. He was astonished at the speed of her leaving. Usually guests waited for their carriage or horse to be called round from the stables and he knew that no such message had been sent.

"Out of my way, fool!" she snapped and did not stop her swift exit until she reached the gravel drive that circled the castle inside the moat.

She could not remember when she had been so insulted! She had been delighted to see William looking so much better, but her comments about now being able to arrange their future to their mutual satisfaction had fallen on deaf ears.

He had cut her off in mid-sentence, shortly after the nurse had left the room, saying that she must forgive him, but his leg was painful and he needed to rest.

She had been shown to a bedroom by that supercilious butler, and spent a restless, uncomfortable night trying to decide what would be the best way of achieving her ambition.

This morning Lady Verity had been sure she could finally agree their engagement.

She had been delighted to find her host well enough to have ventured downstairs to the breakfast room, but before she could even drink her coffee, Lord Melton had been brutally blunt.

"Madam, I humbly apologise if I have by word or deed given you reason to hope for a linking of our names, but although I value your friendship and that of your brother, my heart is already given to another."

Lady Verity had turned away to stop the anger on her face showing. "Indeed, sir. And to whom should I extend my felicitations?"

There had been a long pause and then Lord Melton had murmured, "why to my *angel*, of course!"

Lady Verity swished violently with her riding crop at a clump of daisies that grew in abundance alongside the castle wall. She wished it was this other woman she was hitting!

'His angel, indeed! Who can possibly have sneaked in to steal his affections from me? It must be some local girl, living nearby. I know that no one from London would dare interfere with my plans. Oh, if I could only have five minutes alone with this mealy-mouthed miss, I would show her that I am not a person to be trifled with!'

Her swift steps had brought her round the side of the castle into the stable yard. Yesterday she had left her horse in the care of the groom who rode with her.

Lady Verity had hoped that her obvious love of riding would add to her attraction for Lord Melton. She had chosen her most becoming riding habit, but could have been wearing sackcloth for all the notice he had taken of her!

"My Lady?" Her groom came running out of the stables, brushing crumbs off his jacket. He had been in the middle of a meal, not dreaming that Lady Verity would be leaving the castle so early in the morning.

"Saddle my horse – I am leaving at once!"

"Yes, my Lady. Certainly, my Lady. Will you wait here or – ?"

"Don't chatter, man. Just saddle up that nag my uncle lent me. Quickly!"

She stood, fuming, as he returned to the stables.

"Your riding habit is a lovely colour! Like emeralds."

Lady Verity turned and found a very small child staring up at her. Her hands and face were liberally smeared with grime from where she had been making mud pies in the puddles left from the dawn wash-down of the stable yard.

Lady Verity hastily pulled her dark green riding skirt away from the out-stretched grubby hand.

"Go away, little girl," she snarled.

"My name's Millie Barker," the child said importantly, blithely ignoring the adult's obvious annoyance. She was too young to realise her proper place in life. An older child would never have dared speak to Lady Verity until spoken to. "I live over there in that cottage."

The tall, elegant woman tapped her riding crop against her side, impatience flooding through her. Where on earth was that wretched groom with her horse?

"I fell in the moat, but Miss Edie pulled me out!"

"Really." Why didn't someone come and collect this wretched infant?

"Miss Edie lives in a little room in the stables now, but she's in disguise, she's really a maid at a big house."

Lady Verity's curiosity was piqued. This sounded like a scandal and she was always interested in that.

"A maid in a big house?" she queried with an effort, forcing her voice to be soft and gentle.

She knew nothing about children and although she imagined she would have to provide a husband with one or two some day, she would face that indignity when it arose.

But one thing she did understand was that you caught more flies with honey than vinegar.

The child ignored her and began skipping from one foot to the other through the puddles, oblivious to the muddy water splashing up onto her white apron and Lady Verity's shining boots.

"Look, I can hop!"

"Yes, my dear, and you do it very well. Millie, what big house does Edie work in?"

"I don't know. It's a secret!"

"A secret that she lives in a big house?"

"No, silly! A secret that she's at the castle with her Lady instead of at Donnington Hall."

Verity eyes widened and it was all she could do not to give a gasp of amazement. She pulled a small coin out of the purse she wore at her waist.

"Here, Millie," she purred. "Here's a present for a good little girl. And a clever one too, I am sure. Can you tell me who is the Lady that Edie works for?"

Millie took the coin, her eyes shining.

"She lives in the castle with the Lord. She's pretending to be a nurse, but she isn't really. My father and Miss Edie talk about her a lot. She's hiding. It's a big secret. She's Lady – Lady – Roshnnana."

And with that she skipped away.

Lady Verity stood staring after the little girl, her mind whirling. She had heard all the local gossip from her aunt when she had arrived from London.

Indeed, the whole neighbourhood knew and marvelled about the escapades of Lady Rosanna Donnington. Details of her inheritance, her life in London, her arrival at

Donnington Hall, shortly followed by that important socialite Sir Walter Fenwick and his party, was common news.

Everyone had an opinion. It was the talk of the county. Nothing as exciting had happened around here for years.

Her aunt was a great gossip and had whispered that an announcement of a marriage was expected. The prominent ladies of the neighbourhood were already consulting their dressmakers regarding new outfits and happily reading the latest fashion periodicals for hints on hats and gowns.

But then Lady Rosanna had disappeared and it was rumoured that Sir Walter was scouring the countryside, offering a great reward, hunting everywhere for his runaway fiancée.

'So, that is who has wormed her way into Lord Melton's heart,' Verity muttered as the groom appeared at last, leading the two horses.

'It can only be her. Lady Rosanna Donnington! She was the woman in Lord Melton's room last night! I saw her, spoke to her. If only I had known. How could she do such a thing? Pretending to be a nurse. Talking and touching a man in his bedroom who is not a relation, alone and unchaperoned! It is madness, it will ruin her, but her insanity will help me achieve my goal.'

With the aid of the groom, she vaulted into the saddle and gathered up the reins.

"Are we heading home, my Lady?" the groom asked as he swung himself onto his horse.

"No, not yet. I wish to ride to Donnington Hall. Straight away and as fast as possible."

Smiling, she wrenched the horse's head around and urged him into a trot, saying,

"I have great news for Sir Walter Fenwick! I have found his missing bride."

CHAPTER NINE

Rosanna awoke to the sound of curtains being drawn by a vigorous hand that could only belong to one person.

"Edie, is that you?" she murmured, pushing back the heavily embroidered silk bedclothes and struggling to sit up against the ruffled pillows.

"Yes, my Lady, it's me in person," the little red-headed maid replied.

"Lord Melton sent for me late last night and said I was to take up my duties again immediately. I was that pleased.

"Cor, my Lady, I was glad to get out of that stable room, I can tell you. Phew, the smell of them horses gets into your skin, doesn't it? I've made John Barker duck himself under the pump before he comes into the cottage for his evening meal."

Rosanna smiled at the young girl's chatter. She had missed her so much.

She gazed round her new bedroom in sheer pleasure. With its pretty cream and pink patterned hangings and delicate lace bedding, it was a vast improvement on the dark little room she had occupied when she was just Nurse Robinson, a humble servant.

Things had happened so fast the evening before.

Rosanna had been on the point of going to bed, sad and miserable because of Lady Verity's arrival at Melton Castle when Mr. Digby had knocked at her door.

With a smile and a respectful bow that made her switch from nurse to honoured guest effortless, he had told her that Lord Melton had arranged for her to be moved to another bedroom in the castle, one more suited to her station.

"Thank you, Mr. Digby," she had said gravely, clutching her dressing robe around her. "I am sorry if I – "

"Indeed, Lady Rosanna, we all understand your dilemma," the elderly man responded without a flicker of resentment in his voice.

"It is indeed fortunate that your medical knowledge has helped his Lordship back to full health. At times I feared I would never see that again."

He had led her to a beautiful bedroom, decorated in pink and cream and gold, the curtains and bed linen all embroidered with the M for Melton.

Even though her new bed was far more comfortable than her old, Rosanna had lain awake for hours, wondering in which room Lady Verity was sleeping.

She chided herself for feeling pleased that Lord Melton had taken the trouble to make her position clear to the staff.

'He could do no less, once he knew my true identity,' she murmured into her pillow.

'He has acted to save my reputation and for that I must be grateful. I just wish I could believe he had other motives for my happiness than plain courtesy.'

Now in the bright light of a new day, Rosanna felt herself to be a little happier.

She had made several resolutions in the dark hours of the previous night.

She would return to Donnington Hall, insist that Sir Walter leave and begin her new life as owner of that great estate.

She would start entering her horses for races, make sure that her tenants were happy and busy and deal with the hundreds of appointments that the owner of a great estate had to undertake in Society.

And she would only allow herself to think about Lord Melton once every day!

"Edie, what shall I wear?" she asked as the maid poured hot water into a deep, rose patterned basin.

"All I have with me is my nurse's uniform and aprons. I intend to go back to Donnington Hall today, but I do not wish to leave here wearing that grey monstrosity!"

Edie smiled.

"What about your pale blue morning dress, my Lady? The one with the lace trim."

And with a flourish, she produced the garment from a drawer and laid it over the end of the bed.

Rosanna stared in bewilderment from her to the pretty dress – one of her favourites.

"But how – ?"

Edie giggled, her red curls bouncing under her cap.

"Don't you remember, my Lady? You tore the hem badly one morning when you were walking in the garden at home in London and I said I'd repair it that evening.

"But I clean forgot and when I went to visit me Mum and Dad, I took it with me to do there. Me Mum's a fair old hand at sewing and I knew she'd make a better job of it than me."

"So you had it with you – "

"In me bag all the time when Sir Walter threw me out of Donnington Hall. I pressed it last night and here it is, right as rain and twice as pretty!"

Rosanna jumped out of bed and when she had washed, Edie helped her to dress.

It felt so good to have the soft blue silk against her skin instead of the harsh grey material of the nurse's uniform.

She wondered why the medical authorities would not make nurses more comfortable in their working clothes.

She realised that they had to be serviceable and no one would suggest nurses should wear pale pink or lemon, but Rosanna was sure it would help them to be even more efficient if they were happy with what they wore.

And being happy would certainly be more beneficial for their patients.

"Edie – " she began hesitantly, knowing she had to go downstairs and face Lord Melton, "do you know if Lady Verity Blackwood – ?"

"Left the castle very early this morning, my Lady," Edie said, her eyes twinkling.

Rosanna felt herself blushing but could not help the rush of happiness that flooded through her veins.

Lady Verity had gone! So perhaps she and Lord Melton –

No, she chided herself, you must not think like that. To him you are no more than a neighbour in trouble who has cast herself into his path and is relying on his chivalry.

"She is a very elegant woman, of course," she said, sitting in front of the gold-framed mirror so Edie could comb and dress her long blonde hair.

Edie said nothing.

"She would make a fine Countess for Melton Castle," Rosanna said, pushing her words against the wound to see how much it hurt.

Edie sniffed and busied herself dividing the shiny locks in front of her into sections.

"Fancy is as fancy does, my Lady, as me old Mum says."

Rosanna tried to catch her gaze in the mirror, but Edie studiously avoided her eyes.

She sighed. Edie's old Mum had a saying for every occasion but they never really helped.

"I expect Lady Verity and Lord Melton spent a very pleasant evening together," she tried speculatively, knowing that her maid would have all the castle gossip at her fingertips.

A little smile twitched at Edie's lips.

"Well, I wouldn't know, of course, my Lady, but Peter Simkins, the Earl's valet, did happen to mention over breakfast this morning that Lord Melton retired to his room very shortly after her arrival."

Rosanna threw caution and discretion to the wind.

"But this morning, I imagine they have breakfasted together?"

Edie thrust two pearl headed pins into the finished hairstyle and stepped back, nodding happily.

"I think so, my Lady, but Lady Verity has now left Melton. I saw her in the stable yard with my own eyes."

"I must go downstairs," Rosanna said nervously pushing at the complicated braid Edie had woven from her blonde curls.

"A nice cup of tea will work wonders, my Lady," Edie suggested.

Rosanna found herself smiling as she walked slowly along the corridor and down the great spiral staircase into the grand hall below.

Edie watched her go.

She had a fairly good idea of how the land lay. She had seen the way her Mistress's eyes had widened into deep, dreamy blue pools when Lord Melton's name was mentioned.

Edie gave a little chuckle of contentment.

She knew how she herself felt about John Barker.

Nothing had been said between them, but sometimes words were not necessary. A look, a touch, a certain smile was all that was needed.

But she wondered if Lady Rosanna and Lord Melton were quite as sensible about affairs of the heart as she and her John were. That was the trouble with the gentry. They were always so busy being polite, they could never see what was under their noses the whole time!

Rosanna turned the handle of the breakfast room door with trepidation. Her heart was thumping so hard she was sure the blue silk above it must be moving.

Taking a deep breath, she entered, head held high.

But the room was empty, except for a young parlour maid who brought her the hot chocolate she asked for.

There was no evidence that Lord Melton had already eaten.

The table seemed big and imposing and the breakfast buffet contained various tasty and savoury dishes under the big silver serving covers.

But Rosanna had no appetite for bacon or kedgeree.

She drank her chocolate and nibbled on a piece of toast, wondering what she should do next.

She could not go looking for the Earl, that would be unseemly, but there was also no way she could leave Melton Castle without seeing him.

Just then Mr. Digby, came into the breakfast room.

"If you have finished your repast and are at leisure, Lady Rosanna, his Lordship requests that you join him."

Rosanna swiftly rose to her feet.

"Certainly, Mr. Digby. Is the Earl in his room?"

"No, my Lady. Please follow me."

Puzzled, Rosanna obeyed.

The elderly butler led the way back up the great staircase, but did not stop at the first floor.

Instead he opened a small door and mounted the steep stone steps that circled round the inside of the castle's northern turret.

He was breathing heavily by the time he pushed open a wooden door at the top of the steps and ushered Rosanna through.

She gasped as she realised she was standing just inside the battlements at the top of the tower.

Although it was a sunny day, the wind was blowing strongly and she swayed as a gust caught the skirt of her dress.

Just then a strong hand shot out and grasped her bare arm, holding her steady.

"Be careful, Lady Rosanna. I would not care to see you lying on the stones of the courtyard beneath us!"

She turned to find Lord Melton smiling down at her, his dark hair ruffled by the breeze, the tan already returning to his pale cheeks.

"I thank you, my Lord. Indeed, it is not a fate I would choose for myself!"

"Do you have a good head for heights, madam?"

Rosanna nodded and felt her colour rise as his warm hand slipped away from her bare skin.

"Yes, I believe I do. On my first day at Donnington Hall, Bates, my butler, took me up onto the roof itself so I could look out at my new estate. I felt no fear or giddiness."

"Good. Then come closer to the battlements. You are even higher here than at Donnington, but I am anxious for you to see everything. Don't be afraid."

He held out his hand once more and raising her gaze to his, she smiled and grasped his fingers with her own.

"I would never be afraid when I am with you, my Lord," she murmured and blushed as his grip tightened.

He helped her across the lead flashings on the roof to the side of the turret.

They stood in the embrasure between the battlements and stared out over miles and miles of beautiful English countryside to where the blue hills rose up in folds, many miles away.

For a long minute they stood in silence, the wind whipping colour into her cheeks and tousling the Earl's dark hair into a riot of curls that made him suddenly look younger.

Rosanna glanced at him and felt a little shock run through her.

The great, remote Lord Melton had vanished and in his place stood a young man who seemed to have not a care in the world.

"It makes me very proud – this view," the Earl said softly. "The Melton estate lies to the west as far as the eye can see."

He laughed briefly.

"Indeed, I used to think my father was a boring old man with his endless lectures about the land and caring for our tenants, making sure all our people were well fed and looked after.

"I used to stop listening when he began one of his eternal sermons about our duties and how our ancestors had passed on the torch to us and it was up to me to take it further. Now I look out and realise I feel exactly the same."

"It is a vast responsibility, my Lord," Rosanna replied. "As you know, I have only recently inherited Donnington Hall, which is half the size of Melton, but I am already beginning to appreciate what will be involved."

Lord Melton slipped his hand under her arm, turned her round and led her back across the turret roof to the south side.

He pointed out towards the misty distance.

"There is the river that borders our two estates. And if you look over to the left, just behind that fine clump of oak trees is the Racecourse your late great-uncle built. As you say, Lady Rosanna, a great responsibility, especially for a young lady."

He gazed down at her fine featured face, the rose colour in her cheeks and the blue of her eyes matching the sky above.

Little tendrils of fair hair had escaped their clasp and curled around her neck.

A surge of emotion ran through his veins.

He had never felt like this about a woman before.

A few months ago he had imagined he was attracted to Lady Verity, but now he realised those feelings were just flickers from a candle against the roaring fires he was now experiencing.

Rosanna was everything he had ever wanted, but she was so alone in the world. There were those who would say he was taking advantage of her.

He frowned.

Sir Walter Fenwick wanted to marry her for what she possessed. Would she perhaps think that was his reason too?

He wondered if it was too soon to tell her how he felt.

They were alone, although he had heard scuffed footsteps on the stone steps so guessed that her little red-headed maid was in close attendance, guarding her Mistress's reputation.

Being alone with a man could cause damage to a

single young girl in Society's eyes, even if that man was a Lord of the Realm.

"Would it be presumptuous of me if I asked for your help and advice in the future, my Lord," Rosanna asked hesitantly.

"I know how busy you must be, but if I am faced with a problem I do not know how to solve, it would be helpful to know I could call on you. Or am I being too forward with such a request?"

Lord Melton smiled.

"You are not, Lady Rosanna. I would be delighted to be of help – indeed – "

His voice deepened and the touch of his hand tightened on her arm –

"Even though we have only known each other for a very short time, it would satisfy my heart's desire if you would do me the honour – "

"Oh, look! Look! The flag!"

Rosanna's excited cry broke into his words. She was pointing out across the countryside towards Donnington Hall that could just be seen in the far distance.

Lord Melton gazed out to where a pinpoint of bright colour flapped in the wind.

"Indeed, there seems to be a flag flying from the top of your house, madam. Is this unusual? We fly a flag here at the castle."

Rosanna turned to him, her eyes sparkling with excitement.

"It's the signal to say Sir Walter has left Donnington Hall! I arranged it with Bates, my butler, just before I ran away and came here to be your nurse. He was worried about getting information to me and said he would only fly a flag when Sir Walter had left so I would know that it was safe to go home."

"That is good news indeed, but – "

He smiled down at her animated face.

"I fear bad news as well."

Rosanna frowned.

"How so, my Lord?"

"Why, it means you will be leaving Melton Castle and going home! And my castle will be the darker for your leaving."

Rosanna blushed and stared up into his deep brown eyes for three long seconds before dropping her gaze.

His expression was telling her something she could not, must not believe.

"Your Lordship has been so kind and courteous," she murmured. "I would love to stay and explore the castle properly and see more of your fine estate, but I must go back to Donnington Hall to make sure that everything is all right."

Lord Melton took a deep breath, then stepped back a pace.

She was right. There was a time and place for everything and now he must ensure that this brave, spirited girl was safe in her own home.

He glanced round and, as he had expected, found the little figure of Edie standing in the shadows of the doorway, waiting patiently.

He beckoned and she hurried across to them.

"Edie, run down to John Barker and tell him to saddle up Demon and ready the carriage. Then pack your Mistress's case. We leave for Donnington Hall within the hour."

Edie dropped a brief curtsy, her eyes sparkling.

"Yes, my Lord. At once. Is John to accompany us?"

Lord Melton looked down at the riotous red curls that

were already trying to escape from her cap and smiled.

This one would be just what the serious John Barker needed to bring him back to life. He had been so sad and distant since his wife died.

"Yes, indeed he is. Now, skip to it. There is no time to lose."

Two hours later, one of the smaller Melton carriages was rumbling down a broad country lane with John Barker on the box, handling the reins.

Tethered to the back were the black stallion and Rosanna's grey pony.

The head groom had almost been dismissed for insolence when Lord Melton announced he would ride his favourite horse.

"My Lord, I must plead with you not to ride Demon! He's only been exercised lightly since your accident. He's fresh and on his toes. A real handful. It is too soon, my Lord. Too soon."

"Nonsense, Barker. Mind what you say! My leg is mending well. I am only accompanying the carriage back to Donnington Hall. Not racing at Goodwood, man. If you put a couple slow nags between the traces, I'll ride alongside and doubt if I'll even break into a trot."

Rosanna had been about to climb into the carriage when the discussion broke out.

She reached over to touch Lord Melton's sleeve.

"My Lord, I know I am not a real nurse, but please take John's advice. You will tear your leg open again and all my work will have been in vain!"

Lord Melton's expression changed from stern to indulgent as he glanced down at the small white hand on his arm.

He bowed, silently handed Demon's reins to the

groom and helped Rosanna into the carriage.

He took his place opposite her and Edie scrambled up to sit next to John.

"Cor, John, did you see the way the Earl looked at me Lady? Do you reckon he's thinking he might – ?"

John took off the carriage brake, slapped the reins and urged the horses forward.

"Now, now, Edie. No gossiping." He shot her a severe sideways glance, which was weakened by the glint in his merry brown eyes.

He looked back to his charges and grinned.

"But I've high hopes, lass. Very high hopes!"

Now the carriage rounded a wide bend and Rosanna said,

"Oh, look, my Lord, we are approaching the Donnington Racecourse already. Can we take a moment to visit it?"

"Certainly, my Lady. I would be delighted to inspect it myself. It is some time since I was here.

"Your great-uncle built a marvellous course. The horses benefit from galloping on a circuit rather than just running across the pasture land."

He called instructions to the groom and the carriage pulled up a track and circled round by the gateway into the Racecourse.

John jumped down and helped Rosanna to step out.

Lord Melton followed, opened the gate and together they walked out onto the lush green grass of the Racecourse.

"The ground does not seem too wet, Lady Rosanna, or the sun too hot. I suggest we wander down as far as the first bend. It will do my leg good to stretch it after sitting for a while. We will be in plain view of your maid if you need her."

"I cannot wait to see my beautiful horses racing," Rosanna sighed as they walked along. "It must be such a wonderful sight."

"It is indeed. Speed and strength and majesty all in one animal.

"That is why Demon is such a marvellous horse. He has all those attributes, although he is too heavily built to be a racehorse, which are usually of Arab descent. My stud books can trace all my animals back many generations."

"But you still feel pride in Demon – even if he was the cause of your accident, my Lord?"

Lord Melton laughed.

"I do indeed and take heed, Lady Rosanna, don't be mistaken – I was the cause of my accident, not Demon. My own stupidity and stubbornness in refusing to listen to John Barker on that day ended in the disaster.

"And as you can see, this morning I was almost guilty of perpetuating my bad character traits. I wanted to ride Demon – to impress you, Lady Rosanna! I was determined, once again, not to listen to John.

"I obviously do not learn from my mistakes. My pride will always be my downfall. Thank you for intervening and bringing me to my senses."

Rosanna felt the colour rise in her cheeks.

"Perhaps your bravery should sometimes be tempered by caution," she said gently. "But courage is a quality I much admire."

Lord Melton placed his hand on hers and squeezed it gently.

Suddenly, he looked up and frowned.

As the Racecourse curved away to their left, the trees and bushes grew close to the white railings.

There was a rustling and movement in the

undergrowth and twigs snapped under clumsy feet.

The Earl stopped in mid stride and Rosanna glanced up at him in surprise.

Then she saw the expression on his face and followed his gaze to where the bushes were now parting and four or five tough looking men appeared.

They were an unsavoury group. Dirty and rough, they wore shabby hats pulled down over their faces. One or two had beards and were carrying sticks.

"Stay where you are! Take not another step," Lord Melton shouted. "What do you men want?"

The leader was a tall, thin man with black, broken teeth and a straggling moustache. His eyes glittered under the brim of his hat and he spat before he spoke.

"We've come for the little lady, my Lord. You hand her over, and we'll be away and no one will get hurt."

"You fools, what do you think you're doing. You will all hang for this," Lord Melton snapped, pushing Rosanna behind him.

"I think not, your majesty," leered the leader. "You've got to catch us first. Now, are you going to let the lady go without a struggle, or have we got to start teaching your Lordship a lesson?"

"Lady Rosanna, I want you to start walking back to the carriage – walk don't run."

"I will not leave you, my Lord!"

"Rosanna! Please. I'll hold them off. Get John!"

Rosanna hesitated. She could smell the men now as they drew closer – rank and revolting.

She thought she would die if one of them touched her. And why did they want her? What would they do to her?

But she could not leave Lord Melton here to be attacked by this gang of ruffians.

Just then she heard a shout behind her and hoof beats on the soft grass.

She spun round to see Demon cantering down the track towards them, urged on by John Barker from the distant gate.

"William!" she gasped, formality forgotten in the danger of the moment.

Lord Melton turned, and catching her hand, sprinted towards his horse.

As the big animal slithered to a halt, he grasped the heavy black mane and swung himself up onto his bare back.

Then he leant down and with one heave, Rosanna was sitting behind him, her blue skirt up round her knees, petticoat and stockings showing in a mass of lace.

"Hold on!" Lord Melton shouted as he wheeled the horse around and headed back up the Racecourse at a fast gallop.

Rosanna tightened her grasp around his waist, burying her face for an instant in the warm blue cloth of his jacket.

She had never ridden this fast in her life. It felt as if they were flying, the turf cutting up from the stallion's hooves, the sound of Lord Melton's voice urging him to greater speed.

She chanced a quick glance around, and at that second, she saw the men standing still, not following.

And then, as Demon hurtled towards the carriage and safety, Rosanna's blood froze in her veins.

From behind a bush stepped the unmistakable figure of Sir Walter Fenwick!

CHAPTER TEN

"And you are sure it was Sir Walter you saw, Lady Rosanna?" Lord Melton queried as he and Rosanna walked across the courtyard at the rear of Donnington Hall to inspect the racehorses who were standing in their stalls, being readied for exercise.

Twenty or more heads turned at their approach – black and grey, chestnut and bay, dark eyes questioning, ears pricked and alert.

Lord Melton had asked the same question earlier as the carriage had thundered up the driveway, the horses straining every sinew under John Barker's shouted commands.

But in all the fuss of their arrival – Bates's delight at Rosanna's return and the household's confusion at Lord Melton being her guest, it had been difficult to have a proper conversation.

Rosanna had been shaking from their encounter with the gang of ruffians who had obviously been sent to kidnap her.

It had all happened so fast, one moment she and the Earl had been walking, happy and relaxed, and the next she had been in fear for her very life.

Her butler had told them that Sir Walter and all his party had left Donnington early that morning, apparently heading for London.

He found it hard to believe that such a dreadful crime could have been conceived and put into action by the Knight.

"Indeed, Sir Walter seemed in a very good mood, my Lady, my Lord," Bates said, his face a mass of worry lines as he realised how close Rosanna had come to being spirited away.

"He has been morose for the past couple of days, sitting in the study and insisting that we bring him the best brandy from the cellar.

"But after his visitor arrived early this morning, he cheered up, ate a large breakfast and announced that he and the other ladies and gentlemen would be leaving for London immediately."

"A visitor?" Rosanna queried.

"Yes, my Lady, Lady Verity Blackwood called to leave her card. Very early this morning."

Rosanna had no time to discuss this revelation as she was whisked away by Edie to wash and change her blue dress, which had suffered sadly after her whirlwind bareback ride on Demon.

She had been served a small meal in her room as she lay on her bed and forced herself to face the devil that was haunting her.

She knew she had seen Sir Walter. There was no mistaking that evil face.

Now she repeated it to Lord Melton.

"Yes, it was him. Oh, dear Heavens, he must have planned the whole thing. I am sure he meant for those dreadful men to carry me off and I cannot even begin to think what would have happened to me."

Lord Melton looked very stern.

He reckoned he had a better idea than Lady Rosanna as to what had been in Sir Walter's mind and inwardly he shuddered.

Once he had the girl locked up in some house in London, away from any friends who might want to help her, she would have been totally at his mercy.

A corrupt priest to do his bidding and Lady Rosanna could have become Lady Fenwick before the end of the week.

Rosanna smiled as they reached the horses and lifted her hand to rub a velvety nose as it swung in her direction.

She loved horses so much and could not wait to see these lovely creatures running on her Racecourse.

Just then John Barker appeared.

"I have stabled Demon at the end of the row, my Lord. He's had a good rub down and one of the lads has found me a good thick rug to cover him. He'll be no worse for his mad gallop."

"It was an amazing experience," Rosanna said. "I had no idea a horse could travel at such a speed."

"Perhaps one day you might care to ride out on one of your own racehorses," Lord Melton replied. "Then you will find that although Demon is fast, he is nothing compared to the Arabs you have here at Donnington."

"I should love to try," Rosanna said. "I want to learn as much about my horses as I can and riding them will certainly help."

Lord Melton laughed and leant forward to remove a strand of straw that had become tangled in her hair from where she had been leaning against a pile of bales.

"I can see that I shall face a worthy opponent at the races next year!" he announced.

"May I ask if we are staying here at Donnington Hall tonight, my Lord?" John asked seriously. "I need to send instructions regarding Milly if we are."

Lord Melton hesitated.

He had taken it for granted that they would stay the night, but was he being presumptuous?

"Oh, please stay," Rosanna pleaded. "There is so much to discuss. You did say, my Lord, that I could always call on you for help and advice."

The Earl smiled down at her.

"Of course. John, send word to Melton that we will be staying at Donnington tonight."

The groom nodded and walked away.

"My Lord," Rosanna enquired hesitantly. "Could Lady Verity have discovered that I was at the castle and come here to tell Sir Walter? Would she have done such a thing?"

Lord Melton's hand covered hers briefly as she patted the shining neck of the next animal.

He had also been considering this possibility. He realised how upset Lady Verity had been when she left the castle this morning after their difficult and uncomfortable confrontation.

Had she learned in some way that his nurse was, in fact, the runaway heiress?

Surely she would not have deliberately come to Donnington Hall to tell Sir Walter?

No, he could not believe that of George Blackwood's sister. It had probably been a chapter of accidents and misadventure that had alerted Sir Walter to Rosanna's whereabouts.

"Lady Verity would, I am sure, be the soul of discretion," he said firmly. "She is high-spirited, but not spiteful, have no fear of that."

Rosanna bit her lip.

She knew she was young and not very *au fait* with the ways of the world, but she also possessed a keen feminine intuition and that was telling her that Lady Verity was not to be trusted.

But Lord Melton obviously had formed a very different opinion of her, and it was obvious that he was blinded by loyalty to his old friends.

But perhaps it is not just loyalty, she thought with a sinking heart.

Lady Verity had been a close friend for many years. Perhaps Lord Melton had already given her his word regarding their future together!

Rosanna knew that if that were so, nothing would ever make him break it. His kindness towards his make-believe nurse might be just that – kindness.

She blinked back tears and lifted her chin, determined that he would not see how upset she was. The last thing she wanted was this man's pity!

"I am wondering what action to take against Sir Walter," he mused, gazing down at the golden blonde head so close to his shoulder.

"He cannot be allowed to get away with such abominable behaviour. Arranging to have you kidnapped! It is unbelievable."

Rosanna glanced up into the dark brown eyes that could look so stern or so warm, depending on his mood. She frowned.

"I sometimes wonder – do you think he could be mad?"

Lord Melton accompanied her to the end of the stable block. They turned together and gazed back at the contented horses, the sweetly smelling hay baskets and straw bales. All was quiet and calm.

He pulled shut the heavy doors behind them.

"Mad? Bad, more likely, Lady Rosanna," he replied

grimly as they headed back towards the house.

"What will the authorities do?"

"Without real proof? Nothing, I shouldn't wonder. But if I ever catch up with him, he will rue the day he tried to interfere in our affairs."

Rosanna blushed as they moved indoors.

'Our affairs!' he had said. What could he mean? Her problems were nothing to do with him.

But the warmth of his hand on her arm sent little shivers running down her spine and she could not wholly blame the shakiness of her legs on just her traumatic morning.

*

John Barker made his way to the big, sunny kitchen after he had sent a young lad off to Melton Castle with the message from his Master.

The kitchen was strangely empty at this time of day.

Mrs. Bates always took an hour off to put her feet up and have a rest before tackling the dinner menu and the maids used her absence to tend to their own mending and laundry and breathe a little fresh air out in the vegetable gardens.

Edie had been repairing the lace on one of Rosanna's shifts. Now she was sitting at the big, white scrubbed pine table, drinking tea.

She jumped up when John came in, smiling.

"There you are! I thought you might have had to go back to the castle."

John smiled gravely.

"Not without saying goodbye, lass."

Edie reached down a large blue and white mug from the dresser and poured another cup of tea from the big brown pot on the table.

"Here, John, drink this. It's still hot. It'll do you good. My, what a morning. How are things upstairs?"

John sank down into a high-backed chair, stretched out his sturdy, booted legs and drank his tea with a sigh of satisfaction.

"Ah, that's better. I was that dry. Well, we're staying here tonight, that's for sure. I'll be bedding down in the stable block, I reckon, along with the Donnington lads."

Edie sat down beside him, nursing her own cup of tea between her small, capable hands.

"Then you'll be off back to the castle tomorrow, you think?"

John shrugged. "My Master cannot stay here with Lady Rosanna without some type of chaperone in attendance, now can he? Tongues will wag all over the county over today's escapade as it is."

"I liked it at the castle. I'll miss little Milly," Edie said sadly.

"Oh, yes, and what about me?"

Edie tossed back her red curls and grinned at him.

"Oh, I might give you the odd thought now and then, John Barker. Like I will with everyone I met over at the castle!"

John reached out and took her hand in his. They stared down at their fingers, entwined together and sat in contented silence for a while.

"We'll have to make some plans, lass," John said at last. "But I'm not sure when we can – "

Edie placed a finger on his lips.

"It'll all work out, John. Don't you worry. I reckon we'll be living at the same place before the year's out!"

And as he held her hand against his rough cheek, she

wished her Mistress could be as happy as she was at this very minute.

*

After dinner in the fine drawing room of Donnington Hall, Rosanna sat at the piano and touched her fingers gently to the keys.

Lord Melton stood, one arm resting along the high white marble mantelpiece, watching and listening.

"You play very well, Lady Rosanna," he said. "I recall telling you that when you were just lowly Nurse Robinson and performed that little French lullaby for me back at the castle."

Rosanna looked up from the keyboard and smiled.

"I am badly in need of practice, sir, which I believe I told you at the time. I hope to give at least half an hour to my piano studies every day now I am home once more."

Lord Melton kicked moodily at the smouldering coals in the fireplace.

Even though the summer day had been warm, there was a chill in the evening air and the staff had lit the fire.

"So you have definitely decided to make Donnington Hall your permanent home?"

"Yes, indeed. I love it so much. Nothing could persuade me to leave it now. I have no desire to return to London at all. I shall probably sell the house there, or at least only use it for occasional visits to that city."

Lord Melton crossed the room and stood next to her as she continued to play.

Her fingers faltered a little as she became aware of how close he was standing.

He reached over and turned the page of her music for her.

His mouth was only inches from her ear as he murmured,

"I wonder if there would ever come a time when you could be persuaded to leave Donnington Hall? If it perhaps meant living in the same area, where you could keep an eye on all that was happening on your own estate?"

Rosanna gazed up into his dark brown eyes. Her heart was thumping and now her hands were trembling so much she had to stop playing.

He reached down and linked his fingers with hers, pulling her gently to her feet.

"Rosanna – you must know how I feel about you?" he said urgently. "Please give me a sign that you are not indifferent to my advances."

Rosanna gasped, overcome with emotion. She loved Lord Melton! There, she had finally admitted it to herself. And he was saying that he had feelings for her.

But – the beautiful face of Lady Verity swam into Rosanna's mind.

Surely she was the one Lord Melton truly loved? Perhaps he just felt grateful for the nursing help she had given him.

"You are very quiet, my dear," the Earl said now, frowning. "Have I, perhaps, been too presumptuous. If I have alarmed you in any way – "

"Oh, no, my Lord," Rosanna cried. "It's just – what with everything that has happened – inheriting Donnington Hall, Sir Walter's pursuit of me, running away to Melton Castle – and now you say – "

She pulled away from him, not wanting him to see that she was close to tears.

Her heart's desire was standing in front of her, but how could she possibly accept him when she was not sure that his feelings were genuine and not the result of an invalid's attachment to his nurse?

Lord Melton turned and strode to the door.

"I can see that I have upset you, Lady Rosanna. Please accept my deepest apologies. I will not bother you again. I bid you good evening, my Lady."

And with a curt nod of his head, he left the room.

Late that night, Rosanna was still tossing and turning, unable to sleep.

She had stood silently while Edie had helped her undress and even though the maid had tried to talk while she was brushing her hair, Rosanna's pale face and set expression had managed to halt the younger girl's chatter.

'Had a row with his Lordship, sure as eggs are eggs,' Edie thought with a mental sniff. 'Just when John and me thought everything was working out well – for all of us!'

Rosanna sat up in bed, listening as the grandfather clock on the landing nearest to her room spoke the hour of two o'clock.

Moonlight was flooding across the bed, turning everything it touched to silver.

But Rosanna could not see any beauty or think of anything to bring her happiness.

She knew that she loved Lord Melton with all her heart, but if he felt only gratitude and pity for her, then that was no reason to accept his proposal.

How could she compete with someone as beautiful as Lady Verity?

'But I fear he is sadly mistaken as to her character,' she told herself, pulling her robe around her.

'I know it was Lady Verity who told Sir Walter about me. I just know it was!'

She tossed back the bedclothes and paced around her room in a storm of unease.

Lord Melton would leave in the morning and perhaps she would only see him again at social functions – perhaps even at his wedding!

She could feel a real pain in her chest at the thought of having to attend such an event and pretend that she was pleased for the happy couple.

The room seemed stuffy, even with the window open to the cool night air.

Rosanna felt a great desire to go outside, to walk and walk, to escape from all the wild, unhappy thoughts that beset her at every turn.

Oh, how marvellous it would be to saddle up Taffy, her little mare, and ride out into the night, far away from everything and everyone that hurt her so.

Of course that was not possible, but she could at least stroll in the gardens for a while, just until her racing heart and clouded head had returned to normal.

Ignoring the oil lamp on her dressing table, she pulled a heavy woven shawl around her shoulders and slipping out of her room, walked swiftly along the corridor.

Moonlight flooded in through the wide windows, turning the polished floorboards to silver under her feet.

Just as she reached the top of the stairs, a sudden golden flash crossed the silver.

Rosanna paused, puzzled. Yes, there it was again! A flickering golden light coming through the window, as if someone was outside with a lantern.

In two steps she was looking out, realising that from this side of the house, she was gazing down at the stable yard.

For several seconds she could see nothing that could have caused that flash of colour.

Then, as the moon momentarily vanished behind a cloud and the scene below was plunged into darkness, she saw it – a bright glowing light coming from – the stables!

Rosanna felt her blood freeze in her veins. The stables were on fire!

And even as she watched, she heard yells and shouts and the door to the stables was flung open and a man's figure – she was sure it was John Barker – appeared, framed against the glowing reds and crimson of the flames.

Rosanna wasted no time in screaming. She turned and ran back along the corridor, up a little staircase and beat with both fists on the door of the main guest room.

"Lord Melton – Lord Melton – William! Wake up! Help! There's a fire. You must help!"

To her surprise the door was flung open and Lord Melton stood there. Obviously he had only just started retiring for the night and had reached as far as taking off his coat and unbuttoning his shirt.

"Lady Rosanna! What in the world – ?"

"Quick! The stables are on fire. The horses – oh, William, we must save the horses!"

Even as she spoke, more lights appeared downstairs and voices began shouting.

Lord Melton did not hesitate – he vanished towards the stairs, his face grim and set.

Rosanna set off after him, but hesitated, just as Edie came flying along the corridor towards her, her face white, cap missing, her red curls an untidy riot over her brow.

"My Lady! My Lady! A fire. Oh, God, my John's down there – he's sleeping in the stables tonight!"

Rosanna caught hold of the younger girl, forcing her to stop.

"Steady, Edie! John will be fine. He's a brave and

resourceful man. Now quick, find me some shoes. I want to go downstairs but it will not help if I end up with cut feet."

Edie pulled herself together, her training taking over.

"Yes, my Lady. Right away."

"Oh, and Edie, then rouse everyone who hasn't heard. Gather all the maids together in the kitchen and collect as much as you can find in the way of salves and bandages. There are sure to be people burnt before the night is out."

Within a minute Edie had returned with Rosanna's shoes – not the outdoor ones she had wanted, but little blue silk slippers.

But they would have to do, Rosanna thought, slipping them on.

She ran downstairs and outside into the yard to a scene from hell.

Flames were roaring up into the night sky with a sound like a thousand dragons breathing, sparks flying, the roof of the stables were alight now and silhouetted against the flames were the shapes of men fighting to pull terrified horses out of the blazing stalls.

Someone had organised a chain of buckets and as one of the lads manned the stable pump, others passed the water along, trying desperately to quench the inferno.

"Rosanna! Go back indoors. This is no place for you!" Lord Melton shouted at her as he led a terrified horse past, its eyes rolling wildly in its head.

"I must help! These are my horses!" she cried. "Are all the men safe? And what of Demon? Is he out?"

Lord Melton gazed round at the chaos of men and animals. It was hard to think over the roaring of the flames, the flying sparks as straw and hay caught light, sending cascading showers of fire into the smoke filled air.

"All the men are out. The alarm was raised in time.

And yes, I believe Demon is safe. John Barker released him and he galloped off. We'll find him in the morning."

"But no one has been injured?"

"I think we were in time to save the animals, but I am afraid your stables will be destroyed. Now, please, go indoors, I am scared you will be hurt."

Just then John Barker came up, panting, his shirt torn, a great burn across his chest, his face dirty and black with smoke.

"All out, my Lord. Just the pony left, but I daren't send anyone else in for him."

"My little grey pony? Smudger? Oh, no, he cannot be allowed to perish!" Rosanna cried.

He was too important. He had carried her faithfully to Melton and had outrun Sir Walter on that dreadful day when the monster had chased her back to the castle.

"Rosanna! Wait!"

Lord Melton's shout was in vain.

Rosanna had slipped from his grasp and was running across the yard.

Without hesitating, she pulled her heavy shawl over her head and taking a deep breath, stepped into the stables.

The heat took her breath away. She could feel hot cinders burning through the thin soles of her slippers as she stepped cautiously along, past the empty stalls where the straw and hay were burning fiercely.

"Rosanna! Good Lord, come back before you die!"

It was Lord Melton, a horse blanket over his head, tugging at her arm, but she pulled away as they reached the stall where Smudger was kicking and bucking, trying to force the door open.

"We have to save him!" she shrieked, trying to lift the

metal hook from its clasp and gasping in pain as the iron burnt her fingers.

With a curse, Lord Melton snatched the door open and tossed the rug over the pony's head and with one arm round Rosanna's waist and the other tangled in the grey mane, he raced for the door, as the roof gave up its fight against the fire and collapsed behind them in a fiery rage.

Outside in the courtyard, Lord Melton helped Rosanna to the pump and held her hands under the icy water.

"Oh, my little love," he said, a catch in his breath. "How brave you are. But what would I have done if you had perished?"

Rosanna took her hands from the water, the pain of her burns fading as she gazed into the desperate brown eyes in front of her.

"I am so sorry, William," she whispered. "I only thought of myself. I never considered that I might be causing you pain. I only wanted to save the pony – to me he is a faithful friend."

"And I am a new one, but, with all my heart, I would be your best friend from now on, your lover and your husband.

"*Will you marry me, Rosanna Donnington?*"

Rosanna gazed at him, all the love she felt showing clearly on her face.

"You do me too much honour, my Lord," she sighed.

"You called me William earlier," he said, dropping a kiss on her soot streaked forehead.

"William," she said, her lips curving into a smile.

She stared around at the dirty, busy stable yard, the ruined building, the shouting men still pouring water on the hissing remains.

She had always girlishly imagined that when she said

yes to a proposal of marriage it would be somewhere romantic – a rose-garden, a ball, a country walk in the spring sunshine.

She had pictured a vague male figure saying those magical words, but he had always been immaculately dressed in the height of fashion.

The man kneeling in front of her had a dirty face, blackened hands and a torn shirt that would need to be thrown away.

No, this was not what she had imagined, but she knew with a great certainty that she loved this man with all her heart and that he loved her in return.

Lord Melton pulled her gently to her feet and held her close to his heart as if he would never let her out of his sight again.

John Barker approached, hesitating at interrupting them, but Lord Melton nodded at him to speak.

'My Lord, I think you should come and see what we've found."

"John – ?" Lord Melton stared at the man's face and what he read there made him frown.

"Alone, if you please, my Lord. This is no sight for a lady."

"Wait here, my loved one. I will only be a moment."

Rosanna stood, nursing her burnt fingers, curious as to what could be so important.

Edie appeared from the kitchen with Rosanna's heavy travelling cloak.

She draped it carefully around her Mistress, grumbling under her breath at the ruined dressing robe and slippers.

"Edie, *he loves me*. We are to be married!" Rosanna cried, tears of joy sparkling in her eyes.

"Well, anyone could see what his Lordship felt about

you, my Lady," stated Edie stoutly. "But that's still no excuse for you to be out here in the night air in just your night clothes!

"And with your permission, I'll be marrying John Barker and coming to live at the castle as his wife. You'll be needing a new maid, my Lady."

Rosanna clasped her hand, smiling at the cheerful face.

"Oh, Edie, we will be so happy! If only I could drive the whole problem of Sir Walter away, my life would be perfect."

Lord Melton strode back, his long legs eating up the ground. He looked grave as he took Rosanna's hands in his and kissed her burnt fingers.

"You need not fear Sir Walter any more, my darling," he grunted heavily.

"Sir Walter?"

"There is a body in Demon's stall. A body holding an oil lamp. Some timbers fell on him, but he is quite easy to recognise. It is Sir Walter Fenwick."

"Oh, no! How dreadful, but William, what was he doing with a lamp in my stables?"

Lord Melton shook his head.

"I can only imagine that – much as it pains me to think it of a man who professed to love horses – he is to blame for starting the fire!"

Rosanna gasped.

"But surely not on purpose. No one could be that wicked. All those men and boys could have been killed. All those horses!"

Lord Melton looked stern.

"Let us give him the benefit of the doubt, my dearest girl. Perhaps he intended to just steal Demon and somehow the lamp was knocked from his hand into the straw."

Rosanna swayed slightly and his arm tightened around her.

"I am sorry this had to happen. I want nothing to spoil this precious moment for us."

Rosanna took a deep breath. She was free! Sir Walter was dead. And no matter how shocking and terrible that was, she could only feel a sense of relief.

"William," she said, "I beg you not to concern yourself about my sensibilities. We will no doubt face all sorts of difficulties in our lives in the future. I am not silly enough to believe that everything will be roses and champagne. But our love has been forged in the fire of endurance. I truly believe that nothing can touch it now."

And she raised her face for the kisses that he rained down on her lips.

*

On a brisk winter's day, the bells of the old stone church in the village of Melton rang out across the frosty fields and woodlands, joyfully celebrating the wedding of the year.

Lord Melton was marrying Lady Rosanna Donnington and the church was packed with friends and relations.

They watched as the slight, golden haired girl walked down the aisle in a dress of ivory lace, her long veil a cloud so light around her head it seemed as if it would take flight.

Standing at the ancient altar, Lord Melton turned and watched Rosanna come towards him.

He could feel his heart surge with a never-ending love. There she was – his *angel*. His for ever, at last. He had found her and would never let her go.

At his side, Viscount Blackwood, bursting out of his cherry red waistcoat, nervously fingered the rings in his pocket.

George was sad that his sister, Verity, was not present. She had travelled to Baden Baden to take the waters and had sent word that unfortunately she was feeling too ill to travel back for the wedding.

Up in the gallery, Mr. and Mrs. Bates sat with Mr. Digby.

The two elderly men exchanged satisfied glances.

"Sir Leonard would have been so pleased," Mr. Bates whispered and Mr. Digby nodded.

"The Earl's father would have been delighted too."

He chuckled. "Remind me to tell you about Nurse Robinson some day!"

Next to them, Mr. and Mrs. John Barker, who had married only the month before, sat close together.

Edie had her arm around little Milly who did not quite understand what was going on, but was thrilled with the new red ribbons Lady Rosanna had bought her.

Edie dashed away the tears running down her cheeks. This was not a time for crying, but for rejoicing. Love had rescued Rosanna and all would now be well.

"Be glad to get back to the castle," she whispered to her husband as the organ music swelled to a climax through the ancient stone church.

"After this I reckon we'll all be in need of a nice hot cup of tea!"

The words of the tender ceremony continued their stately progress and a delicate gold ring was slipped onto Rosanna's finger.

She raised her eyes to her new husband as he lifted her veil back from her face.

Smiling, he silently mouthed the words, "*I love you so*

much," as the prayers continued.

Rosanna felt a wave of happiness sweep over her. They would walk out of the church as they would spend the rest of their lives – together in their love for each other.

Theirs was a marriage that would last for all eternity.